THE YOUNG TRAVELER'S GIFT

ANDY ANDREWS

WITH AMY PARKER

TRANSIT

a Division of Thomas Nelson, Inc.
www.ThomasNelson.com
www.transitbooks.com

Published in Nashville, Tennessee, by Tommy Nelson®, a Division of Thomas Nelson, Inc.

Scripture quotations are taken from the HOLY BIBLE: NEW INTERNATIONAL VERSION®. Copyright © 1973, 1978, 1984 by International Bible Society. Used by permission of Zondervan Publishing House. All rights reserved.

ISBN: 1-4003-0427-X

Printed in the United States of America
04 05 06 07 QW 5 4 3 2 1

Dedicated to Sara Petty,
who is making such
a difference in the lives
of young people

one

Michael Holder jumped from the hard, wooden bench each time the steel door slammed shut. He wrung his shaking hands, hoping that the next time the door opened, his parents would appear, and this nightmare would finally end. Through the gray, metal bars, he watched the annoying tick of the red hand of the clock—second by excruciating second.

Surely his parents were on their way by now. He had heard the phone call—the officer's terse, no-nonsense explanation of the whole mess.

"Mrs. Holder, we have your son in custody. . . ."

He couldn't imagine what his mother thought when she had heard those words. The rest of the officer's words just swirled around in Michael's head: ". . . an accident . . . he's fine . . . three in the hospital . . . alcohol was found . . . under investigation . . . charged with reckless endangerment . . . hospital . . . alcohol . . . investigation . . ."

Michael so badly wanted to hear his mom's voice on the other end of the line. Had she been asleep? Of course, she had. It was way past midnight. Was she angry? Humiliated? Crying? Why wouldn't she be? She had just received the most dreaded call in the history of motherhood: "Your son is in jail." What call could be worse? At least the your-son-has-been-killed call suggests that your son was innocent, right? At least with that call, a mom could get in the car knowing that her attempt at parenting had been successful, that she hadn't wasted seventeen years raising a son who would just get himself thrown in jail. . . . Michael shook his head. He was a failure. He had failed his mom and dad. He had failed his friends. He had failed himself.

As the clock ticked on, Michael remembered a game he used to play to ease his mind while he was waiting for his parents to pick him up after school or baseball practice. He would close his eyes and imagine what his mom or dad was doing at that very moment. He would think, *It's 3:30. Mom's getting off work. She's walking out of the office, down the sidewalk, across the parking lot, and to her car. Now, she's unlocking the door, getting in, starting the car. . . .*

He would imagine every little detail of his parents' trips, until one of them would pull up beside him and honk the horn, startling him out of his thoughts. The game had always helped to comfort him. Maybe it would at least distract him now. Out of desperation, he began to imagine what was happening back at his house. *Mom's waking up Dad. . . .* His dad had been so exhausted lately—even more than usual. Just last week, Michael had followed his dad up the stairs and was alarmed by the way his father had to stop at the top of the steps to catch his breath. A few years ago, a half-hour game of one-on-one didn't even faze him, but something had suddenly taken its toll on that man.

Now, Mom's breaking the news. They're getting dressed . . . walking to the car. . . . Michael wondered what they had said to each other, or worse—if they had gotten ready in silence. His dad had always been a man of few words. He never said a whole lot—he never needed to. One look from his dad, and Michael knew he needed to straighten up his act. Boy, was he going to get that look tonight!

Slam! This time Michael barely raised his head to look. But he sat up with a jolt when he saw the all-too-familiar figures coming through the door. His mom's plaid, flannel pants and slip-on clogs told Michael that she had barely taken the time to get dressed before running out the door. He could see that she had attempted to apply some make-up, but it had done nothing to hide her puffy, tear-streaked face. He felt another knot in his stomach—Michael couldn't stand to see his mom cry.

He shifted his gaze to his dad, who met his eyes with a blank stare. It was nothing like the disciplinary look Michael had expected. It was a look of confusion, a what-in-the-world-are-you-doing-here expression on his face, as he stared back at his only son. Michael quickly averted his eyes down to his dad's shirt. He had missed a button and the shirt was untucked—nothing like the crisp, formal way he usually dressed. Michael knew his parents would be angry with him, but now, he was afraid it was much more serious than that.

As his parents spoke with the officer, Michael wondered what they would say to *him*. He could handle stern looks from his father and try-to-do-better speeches from his mother. But this? His dad seemed stunned, and his mother already looked as if she'd been crying for days. How would he face them? What would he say to them? How would he explain what had happened?

It had been a little less than two hours since the crash. Two hours that had felt like an eternity. But now that his parents were standing there looking at him, wanting to take him home, it seemed like he had just gotten there. Well, they probably didn't really *want* to take him home. And Michael wasn't really sure he wanted to go. But as soon as the tall, steel bars swung open, he stood and moved toward his parents. They both turned without a word and walked toward the door. When they got to the car, Michael opened the door for his mom. He didn't receive the clumsy curtsey and "thank you, kind suhr" she typically offered in her worst British accent. Michael would usually roll his eyes at her, but now he wanted to hear her goofy impression more than ever.

The ride home was silent. After a few minutes, they turned onto Northfield Lane, where Michael noted each passing tree. He knew them all by heart. They were only six driveways from home. Five, four, three, two . . .

Forcing one foot in front of the other, Michael made his way into the house. Once they were inside, he couldn't stand the silence any longer. "Dad, I—" His dad quickly held up a firm hand and without a word went upstairs.

Now Michael was the one who was lost. He was an old pro at handling his parents when he was in trouble. He could predict their every move, forecast every punishment. But this was bad. Really bad.

After gulping down a glass of cold water, Michael went to his room. He put the glass on his nightstand and collapsed into bed, burying himself under the covers. *What a night,* he thought as he stared at the ceiling.

Michael blinked slowly and opened his eyes to the morning sun. He couldn't remember what time he had finally fallen asleep. At first, he smiled, and then the previous night hit him. A feeling of dread filled his stomach up to his throat.

"Michael, breakfast." The deep voice startled him. His dad was standing at his door. Avoiding his dad's gaze, Michael jumped out of bed, threw on some track pants and a T-shirt, and slowly made his way down the stairs. His mom was sitting at the table, with a cup of coffee in her hands, staring out the window.

one

"Sit down, son." His dad took a seat across from his mom, and Michael took his usual spot between them, facing the empty fourth chair.

At least he's talking to me now, Michael thought as he poured himself some juice.

"Michael, I'm sick," his dad began.

Okay, I take that back. I wish he wasn't talking to me now. Michael looked up at his dad. "What do you mean, *sick?*" he asked.

"The doctor found a spot on my left lung. It's malignant . . . cancer. I'm having surgery on Monday, and I'll be out of work for a while."

Michael was confused. *Why is he telling me this now? Didn't he pick me up from jail last night?? He's not even going to yell at me?* "Dad—"

"Let me finish. Things are going to be difficult for a while. Your mom is going to need your help. You're going to have to carry part of my load around the house. And now we obviously have other problems to deal with, too."

Michael looked at the floor. *Here it comes,* he thought.

"Your car is wrecked, possibly even totaled, and we only had liability insurance, which means that you won't have your car to drive for a while, unless you can pay to fix it."

Michael slowly nodded his bowed head.

"You'll need an attorney for court, and I'll only be getting disability pay until I return to work. It's enough to cover the bills, but not the added expense of an attorney. You'll have to pick up a part-time job for that."

Michael looked up. "But I have track practice! I can't—"

"You can, and you will. You made a choice last night, and today you will begin to face the consequences. You're almost an adult, Michael, and every man must face the results of his decisions." Mr. Holder turned his head and looked out the window.

They all sat in silence. *If this is some sort of discipline trick, it's working,* Michael thought. Then the reality of what his father had said finally hit him.

"Dad," Michael asked in a soft voice, "are you going to die?"

His mother spoke first. "Michael, we don't really know what is going to happen. The doctors are optimistic, but they won't know anything for sure until after the surgery. If that is the only spot, then the prognosis should be very good. If the cancer has spread, then it will be more serious. There'll be chemotherapy, radiation maybe. We'll just have to wait and see."

one

Michael couldn't believe he was having this conversation. How had his life gotten so completely out of control in less than twenty-four hours? None of it seemed real. He wanted to grab his father, hug him, beg for his forgiveness, and promise to make everything right. But he couldn't. He had screwed up too badly this time. There was no way he could fix this mess. He had disappointed his parents at the worst possible time, and they would never forgive him. And why should they?

He choked down his toast and juice, put his dishes in the dishwasher, and headed back to his room.

A half-hour later, Michael's dad was at his bedroom door again. "I was hoping to get the yard mowed and the gutters cleaned out," his dad said.

"Sure," Michael answered and slipped on his tennis shoes.

The day passed slowly. Michael had plenty of time to think about what had happened as he made his clockwise paths around the yard. *I guess even being designated driver can get you in trouble when you're my age. Wait—D.D. is an honorable position, right?? Well, okay, maybe not for a seventeen-year-old whose friends shouldn't be drinking in the first place. But still, I wasn't doing anything wrong. Okay, I did have that bad feeling before I got into the car. But what* was I supposed to do? I had to take them home. I had to. Of course, I didn't know that they had stuffed beer in their shirts, too.

If stupid Mark hadn't thrown stupid Dave's stupid hat out the window, then stupid Chase wouldn't have jerked the wheel for me to turn around! And then I wouldn't have hit that stupid phone pole at forty miles an hour—or however fast we were going. And to top off all of the stupidity, they weren't wearing seat belts! I should have known better. I should have. But what can I do about it now?

And what's going to happen to Dad? What if the cancer has spread? What if he can't go back to work? What's going to happen to us? I need him. Mom needs him.

"Looks good!" Michael's mom yelled from the front porch as he shut down the mower. His mom was holding two glasses of ice water, and she motioned with her head for Michael to come over.

"Here. Take one to your dad," she said, handing him two glasses of water—one with two cubes of ice, just like his dad liked it.

two

On Monday after school, Michael carefully drove his dad's car straight to the hospital. School had been horrible. The other kids stared at Michael as if he had some rare disease, and he could hear them whispering as he walked by in the halls. His teachers treated him like he was delinquent, like those kids who sat in the back of the room throwing spitballs, if they bothered to show up at all.

In the halls and cafeteria, there was also the obvious absence of three very familiar faces. Michael had gotten up the nerve to call and check on his friends Sunday afternoon. Mark and Dave were expected to come home from the hospital on Monday. But Chase had suffered severe head trauma, and they weren't sure if he'd recover completely.

And then to top it all off, Michael had to tell his track coach he was getting a job after school and wouldn't be able to come to practices. Coach Robinson raised an eyebrow. "Son, you know the rule: no practice, no play, right?"

"Yes, sir."

"And you know that if you don't play, they'll be no chance for a scholarship, right?"

Michael kicked a bare spot in the grass. "Yes, sir. I know. It's only temporary."

"Well, I hope so," Coach replied and turned back to face the track.

Michael was crushed. He had forgotten all about the scholarship scouts coming next week. "That's just great," he said to himself. "Another devastating blow to the future of Michael Holder." He blinked away a tear as he turned into the hospital parking lot.

He rounded the corner of the ICU waiting room and found his mom staring blankly at a magazine. "How is he?" Michael asked.

"Oh—Michael, how was school?" She looked relieved to have someone to talk to.

"Great, Mom. How did the surgery go?"

"It went well. Dad's in the ICU, now. He'll be there overnight, just so they can make sure he's stable before moving him to a regular room. We can see him in about fifteen minutes."

"Okay." Michael took a deep breath and sat next to his mom.

At 3:30, a nurse poked her head inside the waiting room. "Holder family?"

Mrs. Holder looked up.

"You can see him now," the nurse announced and motioned for them to follow her.

They approached a heavy, wooden door labeled "Intensive Care Unit." The nurse pulled the shiny, metal handle and allowed Michael and his mom to pass in front of her. "He's in bed four." She pointed to a pulled curtain in the center of the wall. Michael and his mom walked toward him as the nurse explained quietly, "He has an IV, a Pleur-Evac, telemetry, and oxygen, so don't be alarmed at all of the tubes and wires. They're just to help get him back on his feet again."

A *ploor-what?* Michael wondered. *Just hearing her describe it all is alarming enough!* But when he pulled back the curtain, he realized that nothing could be as disturbing as what he saw. His dad—the guy who had wrestled with him, played basketball with him, and occasionally turned Michael over his knee—was lying there, helpless. His face was swollen and pale, his eyes seemed to be plastered shut, and there were tubes everywhere. Tubes up his nose, a tube taped to his arm, and a tube running from his chest to a machine labeled "Pleur-Evac" in blue.

"It helps to empty the fluid from his lungs," the nurse explained, noticing Michael's look of horror.

"Oh, right," Michael answered quickly and turned to look at his dad.

His mom was holding his dad's still hand. A single tear rolled down her face. "Charles, can you hear me?"

His dad's eyes fluttered a bit. "Dee . . . hi, honey," he answered in a weak voice.

Michael walked closer to the bed. "Dad? You okay?"

The man smiled weakly at his son. "I'm all right. Just a little tired."

Michael stood there for a moment, watching his mother and father, not knowing what to say or do. It felt awful, being so helpless. He couldn't take it any longer. He had to leave—now!

"Oh, okay, . . . um, I'll go and let you rest. I just wanted to say hi." Michael began to back out of the room. He looked at his mom. "I'm going to look for a job. I'll be home later."

His mom nodded and turned back to his dad. Michael walked quickly out of the ICU. He filled his lungs with the outside air, thankful to be away from the chemical smells and electronic sounds of the hospital.

He climbed into his dad's car, not really knowing where to start. He'd never had a real job before. He drove down Restaurant Row, as he and his friends called it, and saw "Hiring Servers" on one of the signs. *Might as well try this*, he thought. He turned into the parking lot and went inside. At the hostess stand, a girl his age asked, "How many?"

Michael cleared his throat. "Uh, actually, I'm here to apply for a job."

"Oh, okay," she giggled. "Hang on."

A few minutes later, a guy not much older than Michael emerged from the back wearing a "Manager" nametag and carrying a clipboard. "Hi, I'm Larry. You want to apply for the server position?"

"Uh, yeah. Yes, sir. I'm Michael. Michael Holder." He quickly shook Larry's hand and followed him back to a small office.

"Here, fill this out." Larry handed him an application. "But to tell you the truth, we're desperate. We just need warm bodies. You're not a criminal or anything are ya?" Larry laughed.

Michael stared at the application, and the same question jumped out at him from the paper. "Well, what exactly do you mean by 'criminal'?"

Larry straightened up his smile and peered across the desk at Michael. "I mean, well, that you haven't been convicted of any crimes; you don't have anything on your record. You don't, do you?"

"Um, you see, I . . . I have this stupid reckless endangerment charge pending, but, um, I'm sure after the judge hears the whole story, he'll drop everything." Michael reached to pick up the pen Larry had given him.

"Sure, kid," Larry answered and stood up from his chair. "On second thought, I've got some things to take care of. Why don't you fill out that application in one of the booths and leave it with the hostess. I'll give you a call if we have anything."

"Okay . . . thanks," Michael mumbled. He walked out of the office, dropped the clipboard with the blank application on the first booth he saw, and walked out the door.

He got into the car and clenched the steering wheel. "Now what?" he asked aloud. "NOW WHAT?!?" A passing couple looked over at him and quickened their pace. He turned the key and spun away.

As he drove, he thought about his pale, weak dad lying in the hospital and his mom holding his hand. *How could I let them down? WHY did I let them down? YES, they taught me better. Of course I knew better. But I did it. Did it anyway. And now what? My dad, who has lost all faith in his son, is sick—looks like he's* dying! *And the one time in his life when he needs me—*

"Whoa!" Michael swerved to miss a squirrel running across the road.

"And what's he going to come home to?" Michael was now yelling over the radio. "'Uh, hey Dad, your loser son just ruined his chances for a scholarship because he's gotta pay for an attorney, and now, he can't even pay for an attorney because he can't get a job. Why?! Because he's a CRIMINAL!! Oh, and welcome home, Pops!'"

Tears began to flow down his face. The road was blurry

in front of him, and he strained to see the street sign. *Clark Avenue? I'm way past our street.* But he didn't care. What would he tell his mom if he went home now? He stomped on the gas. The gold and red leaves on the trees blurred as they passed faster and faster.

Why am I even here, anyway? God, why? You see what I've done to my parents. They have zero trust in me now. And Coach Robinson? He's going to give up on me, and I wouldn't blame him. Michael was past his subdivision now, and the road was becoming more narrow and winding. *My friends? Oh, yeah, I put them in the hospital! Even that Larry-the-Restaurant-Manager guy—a total stranger— doesn't even trust me to carry trays of food around his restaurant. What kind of future does a guy like me have? NONE! That's right. None. Why did this all happen to me?*

Michael threw his hands in the air as he approached the upcoming curve. *Hey! A crash got me into this mess. Maybe a crash will get me out!* When he saw the steep embankment, he grabbed the wheel again, but it was too late. "Oh, God! Why me?!"

And then . . . nothing.

three

"Please, son. Get off the floor and come sit in this chair."

"Dad?" Michael opened his eyes and looked into the face of a familiar man, but as his eyes began to focus, he could tell the man was clearly not his father. He was a small, older man whose neatly combed, almost-white hair contrasted with the untidy appearance of his clothes. The sleeves of his dress shirt were rolled up at the elbows, and his red-and-black-striped tie was loosened at the collar. A pair of small, round, but coke-bottle-thick spectacles were perched on his nose, making his clear, blue eyes seem huge.

"Your arrival is quite an inconvenience," the man said.

"So, what's new?" Michael mumbled.

"Excuse me?" The man looked over the top of his spectacles at Michael.

"Nothing."

"Good. Just sit in that chair and be very quiet." Turning quickly, he walked toward a huge, hand-carved desk. Settling himself behind it and picking up a stack of papers, he grumbled, "As if I don't have enough happening right now."

Trying to get a grip on his surroundings, Michael looked around. He was sitting on a big, expensive-looking rug, and his back was against the wall of a fancy, high-ceilinged room. To his left was the hard-backed chair that had been pointed to by the man who was now busily sorting papers across the room. To his right, a globe stood on a pedestal in front of an unlit fireplace.

Easing up and into the chair, Michael said, "I'm so thirsty."

Without looking up, the man replied, "I'll get you something in a bit. For now, please be quiet."

Unable to contain the question any longer, Michael asked, "So, where am I?"

"Look here now!" The man slammed the stack of papers down on the desk and pointed his finger at Michael. "I asked you nicely to be quiet, and I'm expecting you to do it. You are in Potsdam, Germany, a suburb of Berlin, in a free zone presently controlled by the Red army. It is Tuesday, July 24, 1945." The man took a deep breath, appearing to calm down, and reached for his work again. Filing through papers, he said, "There now, sit and chew on that for a while."

Michael propped his elbows on his knees and dropped his head in his hands. *I must be in the hospital. That's where they send kids who try to drive their cars off embankments. A psychiatric hospital.* Michael looked over to the man at the desk. *And who is he? My doctor? If so, he needs to work on his bedside manner. But Germany? Why would he say that? And the Red army? Maybe he's as cuckoo as I am.*

Unzipping his pullover, Michael realized he was starting to sweat. He noticed a water pitcher and some glasses on a small table near the window and walked slowly toward it. Out of the corner of his eye, he saw the man look up, frown, and go back to his work.

Michael tried to pour the water and drink it quietly. He looked out the window and realized he was on the second floor of this building—whatever it was. Below him was the bank of a slow-moving river. But there were no families boating, no children swimming—in fact, as he looked around he saw no one at all. "What's up with that?" Michael muttered as a breeze warmed his face.

Warm air? he thought. *It was pretty chilly when I left the restaurant a few minutes ago.* Then, it hit him. Not only was the outside air warm, but every tree was full of leaves and the grass below him was green. All the trees he had passed on the road had been gold or red. Now they were suddenly green again? *Something is seriously wrong here.*

Michael stuck his head out the window. *Whew, it is hot,* he decided. *So, why are the windows open, anyway? The air conditioning should be running full blast.*

Walking toward his seat, Michael scanned the walls for a thermostat. He didn't see one. The only thing he saw was an old heater that someone had stuck in the fireplace. *Not that that old thing would do anyone any good,* he thought. *It's so old it looks like it would've been made in . . .* Michael stopped. He whispered aloud, ". . . the 1940s."

He stood up suddenly and faced the man behind the desk. The white-haired man looked up and slowly pushed his work to his side. A slight smile on his thin lips, he leaned back into his chair, crossed his arms, and peered curiously at Michael.

Michael's mind raced. *Potsdam . . . why does that weird*

name sound so familiar? I've never been to Germany, and I've certainly never been to Potsdam. Wait—Potsdam! He suddenly remembered that just weeks before in American History, Miss Collins had gone on and on about Potsdam, the site of some war conference. After the conference, they had made the decision to drop the atomic bomb on Japan. That was during World War II.

A sudden case of the chills ran through Michael's body as he remembered the president who had attended that conference and the black-and-white photo in the history book. He sat down hard and tried to catch his breath. "You . . . you're President Truman."

"Yes," the man said, "I am. Although, at the moment, I would give anything to be almost anyone else."

"I can't believe this! We were just studying you! You're known for giving people a hard time," Michael added.

Truman grimaced. "I never give anyone a hard time. I just tell the truth, and they think it's a hard time."

Removing his glasses, he rubbed his eyes and said, "Obviously, I'll not be getting any peace from this point on, so we might as well go ahead and talk." Putting his glasses back on, he rose and came out from behind the desk. "By the way," he said, "why *not* you?"

"Sir?" Michael was confused by the vague question.

"Why . . . not . . . you?" Looking into Michael's eyes, Truman enunciated the words carefully, as if he were speaking to a child. "I believe that is the last question you asked before you arrived."

Michael frowned, trying to remember. "I was in an accident, I think."

"Yes," Truman said, "that's sometimes how this happens. And the last question a person asks is often, 'Why me?' Of course, 'Why me?' is a question great men and women have been asking themselves since time began. I know the thought has occurred to me more than once during the past few days. What's your name, son?"

"Michael Holder. Am I . . . am I okay?"

"Well, Michael Holder, if you mean, 'Am I dead?' the answer is no. If you simply mean, 'Am I okay?'" Truman shrugged. "I'm not sure. I've never been given any information on how these things turn out."

Suddenly, Michael relaxed. He smiled and nodded his head. "I get it. I'm dreaming, right?"

"Maybe you are," the president said, "but, Michael, I'm not. And even if you are dreaming, that's not a problem. For centuries, dreams have been used to communicate instruction and direction to people of purpose—great men and women. God used dreams to prepare Joseph for his future as a leader of nations. He gave battle plans to Gideon in a dream. Joan of Arc, Jacob, George Washington, Marie Curie, and the apostle Paul were all guided by their dreams."

"But I'm nowhere near a 'great man,'" Michael said. "I'm nothing like any of the people you've mentioned. I've messed everything up. I'm certainly no apostle Paul. I'm not even sure I believe in God anymore."

Truman smiled and put a hand on Michael's shoulder. "That's all right, son," he said. "He believes in you."

"How do you know that?" Michael asked.

"Because," Truman answered, looking directly at Michael, "you wouldn't be here if He didn't. Sometimes, someone is chosen to travel the ages, gathering wisdom for future generations. It's as if God literally reaches down and places His hand on a shoulder, and in this case," the president peered over his glasses, "it was *your* shoulder."

A sharp knock at the door interrupted them. Without waiting for a response, a stocky man strode into the room. "I'm sorry to barge in, sir," he said, his eyes surveying the room. "I thought I heard you talking to someone."

"No, Fred," Truman said as he looked directly at Michael,

"no one here." Then motioning toward the door with his hand, he said, "Will you see that I'm not disturbed?"

"Of course, Mr. President," Fred said as he slowly backed out, a concerned look on his face. Still looking around, he added, "I'll be escorting you to the conference room within the hour, but if you need me before then—"

"You'll be right outside," Truman said as he ushered the confused man from the room, "and I won't hesitate to call for you. Thank you, Fred."

When the president closed the door, Michael asked, "He can't see me?"

"Apparently no one can," Truman replied. "No one, that is, except the person you came to visit. Of course, that makes me look a little crazy," he said with a grin, "in here, all alone, talking to myself. Fred Canfil is my special bodyguard. He's temporarily assigned to the Secret Service, and I've grown rather fond of him. He must think the stress has finally gotten to me."

Quickly, he wiped the grin off his face and continued, "But I don't understand why anyone would find it strange. I have ample reason to be talking to myself, with everything that's going on here." Truman cocked his head and looked at Michael from the corner of his eye. "It is curious how you people always seem to show up during critical points in *my* life."

"This has happened to you before?" Michael asked.

"Yes," Truman said. "The first time was the night Roosevelt died. I was alone in the Oval Office, and a young man about your age appeared out of nowhere. Fred came busting through the door—almost gave me a heart attack. It was strange that no one could see the boy but me."

"So, what did he want?"

"He was having trouble deciding whether or not to finish college."

Michael couldn't believe it. "That's not a big enough problem for the president of the United States!"

"What are you here for?" Truman asked.

Michael shrugged his shoulders and looked down at the floor. "I don't know. I really don't know."

"Well," the president said as he moved across the room, "at least that young man had a question."

"So, what did you tell him to do?" Michael asked.

"I didn't tell him to do anything," Truman replied. "That's not my part in all this. I offer my point of view. The ultimate outcome of anyone's life is a matter of personal choice." The president continued, "I was evidently his second visit. He had just spent an hour or so with Albert Einstein."

"Wait." Michael looked up. "I'll be going somewhere *else* after this?"

"Yes, you will," Truman answered. "Several different places actually, but don't worry. They will be expecting you."

"So . . . you knew I was coming?"

"I was informed in a dream the other evening," Truman said. He walked behind his desk and opened the right top drawer. Removing a folded piece of paper, he handed it to Michael and said, "I was instructed to prepare this for you. This is why you are here. It is one of the Decisions for Success. You will receive seven in all. Keep it with you, and read it twice daily until it is committed to your heart. For only by committing this principle to your heart will you be able to share its value with others."

Michael carefully began to unfold the page. "No, wait," the president said as he put his hands over Michael's. "Don't read it yet. You must wait until our meeting is finished. After you read those words, you will immediately travel to your next destination. Amazing, actually. You read the last word and—bang!—you're gone!"

Michael reached over and started spinning the globe,

stopping it on the United States. "Do you know my future?" he asked.

"Nope," Truman said. "Can't help you there. And I wouldn't if I could. Your future is what you decide it will be. Now you, on the other hand, could probably tell me mine." Michael opened his mouth to speak, but the president held out his hands as if to ward off the words. "Thanks, but no thanks. God knows, there are enough influences coming to bear without you telling me what I already did!"

"Let me get this straight, now. You say that my future is what I decide it will be?" Michael began. "I don't know about that. I certainly didn't decide to be in the situation I'm in now. I've been a good friend, a pretty good son, a dedicated team player, and a decent student. But now my three best friends probably hate me, my parents don't trust me, my dad's really sick, and I'm off the track team, which means I won't get the scholarship I need to go to college."

"Michael, we're all in situations of our own choosing. Even with the things we can't control, we have a choice in how we react. Our thinking creates a path to either success or failure. However, by not taking responsibility for our present, we crush the possibility of an incredible future that might have been ours."

Michael shook his head. "I don't get it."

"I am saying that outside influences are not responsible for where you are mentally, physically, spiritually, emotionally, or financially. You have chosen the path to your present destination. The responsibility for your situation is yours."

Michael jumped up from his chair. "No!" he cried. "I didn't *mean* for this to happen! I was trying to *help* by driving my friends home that night. Everything just went all wrong. It's not . . . my . . . fault!"

Truman placed his hand on Michael's back. "Sit down," he said softly. He pulled a chair around to face Michael, who was now trembling with anger and confusion. "Look here, son. It is not my desire to upset you, but with the limited time we have been given together, truth will have to come before tact."

The president leaned forward and took a deep breath. "Listen to me. You are where you are because of your thinking. Your thinking controls your decisions. Decisions are choices. In the past few years, you have made choices that will affect the rest of your life. You have chosen your friends, how highly to regard your parents, whether to study or go to a party on a Friday night. You began making choices years ago that led you to your present situation. And you walked right down the middle of the path every step of the way."

Truman paused. He pulled out his handkerchief and wiped his brow. Michael's head was hanging, his chin on his chest. "Michael, look at me," the president said. "The words 'It's not my fault!' should never again come from your mouth. The words 'It's not my fault!' have been symbolically written on the gravestones of unsuccessful people ever since Eve took her first bite of the apple. Until a person takes responsibility for where he is, there is no way to move on. The bad news is that the past was in your hands, but the good news is that the future, my young friend, is also in your hands."

As the president leaned forward to touch Michael on the shoulder, he was interrupted by three quick knocks on the door. "Mr. President," came a voice from the hall-way. It was Fred Canfil again. He opened the door slightly and said, "Five-minute warning, sir. I'll wait for you out here. Mr. Churchill and the Russian are already making their way to the conference room."

"Thank you, Fred." Truman chuckled. Once the door closed, he said, "It seems my bodyguard doesn't care very much for Mr. Stalin. Come to think of it, neither do I. But I suppose he's a necessary part of this process." He stood up and began rolling down his sleeves and buttoning the cuffs.

Michael saw the president's jacket hanging over the back of the desk chair and went to retrieve it.

"What will you do?" he asked.

Truman buttoned his collar, straightened his tie, and looked over at Michael. "Let's not play games here, son. You've studied your history. I think we both know what I'm about to do. Do I want to do it? Do I want to deploy this . . . this bomb? Of course not!"

He walked quickly to his desk and gathered several notebooks. Suddenly, he put them down again and faced Michael. "I don't have any idea what you know about me." He paused. "I mean, I don't know what people say about me in the . . . ah . . ." He wriggled his left hand at Michael as if he couldn't come up with the words he wanted to say. "I don't know what they say about me where you come from. For all I know, history books are full of what I eat or how I dress, and frankly, I don't care. But let's get something straight between you and me. I hate this weapon, okay? I'm scared of it and concerned about what it might mean for the future of our world."

He stared blankly at Michael for a moment. It was as if he was seeing something in his own future, and it frightened him. Shaking his head to clear his thoughts, he said, "Still got the paper?"

"Yes, sir." Michael held up the folded page that had never left his hand.

"Well, then," the president said with a smile, "go ahead and read it." He walked to the door, opened it, and was about to go through when he paused, turned, and said, "Michael?"

"Sir?" Michael answered.

"Good luck, son."

"Thank you, sir," Michael said.

Truman turned to leave, but again he reached back in and shook Michael's hand. "And just because I use the expression 'good luck' doesn't mean that luck has anything to do with where you end up." And with that, the president of the United States closed the door.

Michael was now alone in the large room. He walked slowly to the desk and sat down in the big, leather chair where Truman had been only moments before. He slowly unfolded the paper and began to read.

The First Decision for Success

The buck stops here.

From this point forward, I will accept responsibility for my past. I understand that in order to have wisdom, I must accept responsibility for my own problems, and that by accepting responsibility for my past, I free myself to move into a bigger, brighter future of my own choosing.

Never again will I blame my parents, my friends, my teachers, my coach, or my boss for my present situation. Neither my education nor lack of one, my genetics, or the ups and downs of everyday life will affect my future in a negative way. I will look forward. I will not let my history control my destiny.

The buck stops here. I accept responsibility for my past. I am responsible for my success.

I am where I am today because of decisions I have made. My decisions are controlled by my thinking. I will begin to change where I am today by changing the way I think.

My thoughts will be constructive, never destructive. My mind will live in the possibilities of the future and not in the problems of the past. I will choose to be around others who are working and striving to bring about positive changes in the world. I will never seek comfort by being around those who have decided to be comfortable.

When I have the opportunity to make a decision, I will make one. I understand that God did not give me the ability to always make right decisions. He did give me the ability to *make* a decision and then *make it right*. When I make a decision, I will stand behind it. I will put my energy into making the decision. I will not waste my time on second thoughts. My life will not be an apology. It will be a statement.

The buck stops here. I control my thoughts. I control my emotions.

From now on, when I am tempted to ask, Why me? I will immediately answer: Why *not* me? Challenges are opportunities to learn. Difficulty is preparation for greatness. I will accept this preparation. Why me? Why *not* me?! I will be prepared for something great!

I accept responsibility for my past. I control my thoughts. I control my emotions. I am responsible for my success.

The buck stops here.

four

As soon as Michael read the final words of the note, he looked up. The office turned and shifted; the edges of the room became lower than its center. The desk seemed to stretch and curve. He stood up, pushed the chair away, and stepped toward the window. He never made it. Suddenly dizzy, Michael's knees buckled, and he landed face first on the floor. He reached out to catch himself, but his hands pushed through the floor as if it weren't even there. The rest of his body followed his hands into complete darkness.

four

Almost instantly, like he had fallen through the floor into a room below, Michael was on his feet, alert and unharmed. He was in a large, ornate room that was the size of his high school gym, but much, much older. He was in the middle of a group of people who were pushing for a position to see something going on at the front. The men weren't wearing shirts and were deeply suntanned. The women wore robes of brightly colored cloth, and their extremely long hair was rolled into ropes and twisted down their backs.

Without warning, a gong was struck. Michael grabbed his ears and watched every man and woman around him as they stopped talking, fell to their knees, and lowered their heads. Stunned, Michael just stood there, and suddenly he had a clear view of the room.

Directly in front of him were six steps. On each side of the steps were statues of lions carved from dark marble. But they were nothing compared to the sight at the top of the steps. Standing alone in the center of a granite pedestal was a throne made of ivory and trimmed in gold. The back of the chair was rounded at the top and had armrests on each side. Two more lions, these also made of gold, stood silent watch beside the throne.

The gong sounded again, and a man near the throne walked quickly to a curtain and parted the cloth. Stepping through the open space was the most radiant human being Michael had ever seen. He wore a robe of brilliant turquoise. Rubies and gems of every sort were sewn into the hems and sleeves of the garment. Around his arms and neck were bands of solid gold. The crown on his head, also made of gold, was dusted with small diamonds. Michael, the only person still standing, stared open-mouthed at this awesome figure.

He was a large man. Even in sandaled feet, he appeared to be a foot taller than Michael. His thick, dark hair was shoulder length, parted in the middle, and seemed to be held in place by the heavy crown. Circling to the front of the throne, he sat down and said simply, "Let us begin."

Immediately, the crowd leaped to its feet, and the argument around the throne began again. As Michael got closer, he could hear the angry voices of two women growing louder.

"He is mine!" one screamed.

"No, no!" cried the other. "You are a thief!"

Michael made his way to the front as the crowd grew wilder, taking sides with the women and shouting insults at them. Michael found it oddly similar to those after-noon talk shows where people fight out all of their personal problems. But somehow, Michael felt, this was much more real.

"Silence," the man on the throne commanded, and a hush passed over the people.

Michael moved to the edge of the steps, where he could clearly see the two women and the throne above them. No one seemed to notice him slipping through the crowd. He felt invisible. Seeing the women clearly for the first time, he noticed that one of them held a newborn baby.

Every eye in the room was looking toward the throne. Michael felt like he was the only one breathing. Then, with a movement of his hand, the man on the throne indicated the second woman, who was alone, and said softly, "Tell me your story."

The woman bowed and said, "Your Majesty, this woman and I live in the same house. Not long ago, my baby was born at home. Three days later, her baby was born. No one was with us. Last night, while we were all asleep, she rolled over on her baby, and he died. Then while I was asleep, she got up, took my son out of my bed, and put him in her own. Then she put her dead baby next to me."

The crowd murmured as she continued, "In the morning, when I arose to feed my son, I saw that he was dead. But when I looked at him in the light, I knew he was not my son."

"NO!" the other woman shouted. "He *was* your son. My child is alive!"

"The dead baby is yours," yelled the woman who told the story. "You are holding *my* child. *My* baby is alive!"

The women argued back and forth until the king raised his hand and silenced them again. Michael saw the king look into the eyes of each woman. In a measured tone, he commanded an attendant, "Bring me my sword."

Michael watched without moving as the sword was brought from behind the curtain. It was nearly five feet long—shining silver with a golden handle. The king took it in his hand, stood up, and said, "Bring the baby to me. I will cut him in half. That way, each of you can have a part of him." A guard approached the two women and seized the infant. He placed the baby on a stone table before the king, and the king raised the sword as if to strike.

"Wait! Please don't kill my son!" screamed the woman standing alone. She fell to her knees. "Your Majesty, give him to her, but don't kill him!"

"Go ahead. Cut him in half," the other woman snarled. "Then neither of us will have the baby."

The king put down his sword and said softly, "Give the child to her," pointing to the woman who was on her knees, weeping. "She is the real mother."

As the woman's tears of despair turned into tears of joy, the baby was placed in her arms, and the crowd cheered. Michael yelled and clapped right along with them. When the king rose from his throne, the people knelt to the ground once more, leaving Michael standing alone. As the king walked toward the curtain, he paused, turned, and looked directly at Michael as if to say, "Are you coming?"

Michael caught the look and quickly followed him up the steps. Passing through the curtains, he entered a smaller but more amazing room. Gold shields crossed with silver spears lined the walls. Pillows of linen and tanned skins were scattered in the corner near a low table covered with food of every kind. Light poured through the windows that were accented in ivory and gold.

Michael came into the center of the room, but the two attendants guarding the room didn't notice him. The king finished his conversation with a man Michael heard him call Ahishar, and then he moved to recline on the pillows at the table. Still talking to Ahishar, the king added, "Please go now and instruct all the attendants to leave the hall."

Ahishar was shocked. "But, Your Majesty, it's not safe for you to—"

"I prefer to be alone," the king interrupted. "Thank you for your concern, but it is unnecessary at this time." Ahishar bowed and left, motioning the attendants out after him.

Finally alone, Michael and the king stared curiously at each other. The king spoke first. "Do you know where you are?" he asked with a smile.

"Yes, sir," Michael answered slowly.

"Do you know who I am?"

"Yes, sir, I do. You are King Solomon, sir. I recognize the story. . . . I mean, I remember what happened out there." Michael took a breath. "What I am trying to say is that I remember that story from when I was little."

Solomon smiled. "No matter," he said. "Are you hungry?"

"Yes, sir," Michael replied.

"Then, please, join me." Solomon pointed to a big pillow, and Michael quickly sat down. "You see before you the finest food available anywhere in the world. The food, and anything else you might need, is yours for the asking."

"Thanks," Michael answered, reaching for some fruit. "By the way, my name is Michael Holder."

"Two names," Solomon noted. "And still, you speak my language well. Have you been schooled in Hebrew, or is your tongue a surprise to you?"

Michael, a bit confused, reached up and touched his tongue. "Oh! You mean my language. I was amazed that I could understand every word being spoken when I got here, and I'm even more amazed that I can speak to you now. I mean, yeah, I made As and Bs in Spanish, but speaking fluently in an ancient language—that's unbelievable!"

Solomon chuckled. "It is not so ancient to me, my friend, but I do understand your astonishment. Wherever you travel on this unusual journey, you will find that your mouth and ears have been granted a special ability to communicate and comprehend so that you may be able to understand the gift with which you are being entrusted."

"A gift?" Michael asked.

"Yes, the scrolls," Solomon answered. "I prepared this one for you only this morning." He gently placed his hand on a thin piece of leather that had been tightly wound around a small, wooden rod. It is the message that was placed in my heart for you. This is merely a part of what must be ingrained in your life before you will be able to pass the gift to others."

"Hang on. How am I supposed to pass this . . . this gift to anyone?" Michael shook his head.

The king grinned as he reached for a bunch of grapes. Plucking one from its stem, he placed it in his mouth and said thoughtfully, "That is something you may not know for yet some time. Then again, the answer could be revealed to you tomorrow. Jehovah will move mountains to create the opportunity. It is up to you to be ready to move yourself."

Michael leaned toward the king. "I think I get it. You mean I have to be ready for what's coming." Solomon nodded slowly. "Then how do I prepare for something when I don't know what it is *or* when it will happen?"

"Seek wisdom," the king said simply.

Michael had to stop himself from rolling his eyes. "Okay, I know I'm not stupid, but I'm not catching on here. How do I *seek wisdom?*"

"The answer I have for you will not help your frustrations with me," the king replied and then paused. "My answer is to seek wisdom."

Michael couldn't believe what he was hearing. *Even the*

wisest king in all of history talks in circles just like every other adult, he thought.

As if the king had heard Michael's thoughts, he spoke, "Michael, you have a condition common to most people. You hear, but you do not listen.

"Seek wisdom. *Seek* wisdom. Wisdom waits to be gathered. She cannot be bought or sold. She is a gift for those who don't give up, and only those who truly look will find her. The lazy man—the stupid man—never even looks. Wisdom is available to many but found by few. Seek wisdom. Find her, and you will find success and contentment."

"Well," Michael said, "I certainly don't have success or happiness in my life right now."

"That is all in the past," Solomon noted. "Even the present is constantly becoming the past—now . . . and now . . . and now." He snapped his fingers as he talked. "The past will never change, but you can change the future by changing your actions today. It is really very simple. We are always changing. We might as well guide the direction in which we change."

"How do I guide my direction?" Michael asked.

Solomon rose to his feet and began to walk around the room. Clasping his hands behind his back he said, "Your parents—are they concerned about the types of friends you choose?"

Michael did roll his eyes this time. "Yes."

"Why do your friends concern them?" Solomon asked.

"Well," Michael began, "they say if I hang around with people who do bad stuff, I'll do bad stuff too. But that's not true. I make my *own* decisions."

"So, your friends don't influence the direction of your life?" Solomon continued.

"No," Michael answered quickly, but remembering the situation he had left at home, he added, "Well, okay, maybe a little."

"Exactly!" the king said with excitement. "The answer, of course, is that we are always influenced by those with whom we associate. If a man keeps company with those who curse and complain, he will soon find curses and complaints flowing like a river from his own mouth. If he spends his days with the lazy—those seeking handouts—he will soon find his finances in disarray. Many of our sorrows can be traced to relationships with the wrong people."

Michael jumped to his feet and wiped his hands on his jeans. "So this is an important step in seeking wisdom?"

"Possibly *the* most important step," Solomon responded.

"Guard your associations carefully, Michael. Any time you tolerate the average in your friends, you become more comfortable with the average in your own life. If laziness isn't an irritation to you, it is a sign that you have accepted it as a way of life. You saw Ahishar as you entered, did you not?"

Michael nodded.

"I have many men with whom I keep counsel. If it is important for a king to be careful in his choice of friends, would it not also be important for you?"

Michael walked over to one of the gold shields on the wall and ran his finger across the textured surface. "You are the wisest man in the world," he said, "and obviously the richest. So why do you need the advice of other men?"

Solomon smiled patiently. "Only a fool refuses the counsel of wise men. There is safety in counsel." Solomon moved to the table and picked up the scroll. Placing it into a fold of his robe, he motioned to Michael. "Follow me."

As Solomon exited the interior room, he held the curtain open for Michael to pass. Michael stepped under Solomon's arm and said, "I should be holding the curtain for you. After all, you are the king!"

Solomon laughed. "Thank you, but I appreciate the opportunity to serve *you*. When a king begins to act like a king, it is not long before someone else is king! Serving is a way we can place value on one another. A wise man is a server."

As they walked into the great hall, Michael pointed to the throne. "May I touch it?"

"Certainly," Solomon replied. "Sit in it if you wish. It is only a chair."

Michael touched it carefully and eased himself onto the throne. With a grin, he said, "I feel very small sitting here."

"As do I." Solomon chuckled. Then added seriously, "The responsibility that comes with leadership is humbling. When I sit there, I am grateful for the lessons of my father. He has been dead now for many years, but his lessons still guide me."

Michael remembered his own father in the hospital. *What lessons has he tried to teach me? I hear him, but do I listen? . . .*

Solomon interrupted his thoughts. "It is time for us to part, my friend," he said, handing him the scroll. "I hope that our time together will bring more understanding to your life's journey. I can do nothing to help your struggles and would not if I were able. Battle the challenges of your present, and you will unlock the prizes of your future."

"Thank you, Your Majesty," Michael answered.

"Of course," Solomon replied. He smiled and bowed slightly. "It has been an honor to assist you. Farewell."

Michael watched King Solomon until he disappeared through a doorway flanked by guards at the opposite end of the room. Slowly, he slid back onto the throne and smoothed the king's words onto his lap.

The Second Decision for Success

I will seek wisdom.

Knowing that wisdom waits to be gathered, I will actively search for her. My past can never be changed, but I can change the future by changing my actions today. I *will* change my actions today! I will train my eyes and ears to read and listen to books and recordings that bring about positive changes in my personal relationships and a greater understanding of my fellow man. No longer will I bombard my mind with materials that feed my doubts and fears. I will read and listen only to what increases my belief in myself and in my future.

I will seek wisdom. I will choose my friends with care.

I am who my friends are. I speak their language, and I wear their clothes. I share their opinions and their habits. From this moment forward, I will choose to associate with people whose lives and lifestyles I admire. If I associate with chickens, I will learn to scratch at the ground and squabble over crumbs. If I associate with eagles, I will learn to soar to great heights. I am an eagle. It is my destiny to fly.

I will seek wisdom. I will listen to the counsel of wise men.

The words of a wise man are like raindrops on dry ground. They are precious and can be used for immediate results. Only the blade of grass that catches a raindrop will prosper and grow. The person who ignores wise counsel is like the blade of grass untouched by the rain soon to wither and die. When I counsel with myself, I can make decisions only according to what I already know. By counseling with a wise man, I add his knowledge and experience to my own and dramatically increase my success.

I will seek wisdom.

I will be a servant to others.

A wise man will develop a servant's spirit, for that attracts people like no other. As I serve others, their wisdom will be freely shared with me. Often those with a servant's spirit become wealthy beyond measure. Many times, a servant has the ear of the king, and a humble servant often becomes the king because he is the popular choice of the people. He who serves the most, grows the fastest.

I will be a servant to others. I will listen to the counsel of wise men. I will choose my friends with care.

I will seek wisdom.

five

I will seek wisdom. After reading those words, Michael closed his eyes and tensed his body, preparing for the dizziness he had felt before. This time he was ready. At first, nothing happened, but just as he was about to relax, he opened his eyes to see his fingers literally sliding through the ivory throne as if it were air.

The next moment, Michael heard the loudest noise he had ever heard in his life. *Thunder?* he thought and looked toward the sky. Before he could answer himself, a hand slammed into his chest, grabbed his shirt, and yanked him to the ground.

"Get down, man!" the owner of the hand yelled as he pushed Michael's face to the dirt. "I don't know if you can get shot, but let's not find out, okay?"

Michael turned his head in panic and stared at the man who had pulled him down. He was older than Michael—maybe mid-thirties, with dark brown hair and a long, bushy mustache. He wore dark blue trousers with a faded yellow stripe down the side and a shirt that was beyond dirty. The clothes, like their owner, looked as if they had not been washed in a month. He was rather thin and probably tall. It was hard to tell because he was laid out on the ground firing an old rifle over a pile of rocks. The sound Michael thought was thunder was actually the sound of cannon fire.

Bullets whined off the rocks like swarms of angry bees. All around him, Michael heard howls of anger and pain. Cannons, rifles, and soldiers combined to create a sound so loud that Michael had to scream to be heard. That wasn't a problem. In fact, at the moment, it was the most natural thing in the world to do. He was terrified. He grabbed at the man's shoulder and cried, "Who are you?"

"Chamberlain!" the man yelled, reloading his rifle from the muzzle. "Chamberlain of the Twentieth Maine!" And he turned to fire again.

"Where are we? What's going on?" Michael had never been so scared in his life.

"Stay down!" Chamberlain shouted. "No time now. We'll talk later—I hope."

Chamberlain continued to fire downhill, reload, and shout encouragement to the men around him. Michael saw that they were almost at the top of a steep, wooded hill that sloped down and away from them. Beyond Chamberlain, Michael witnessed scenes of war and death that were far worse than the gruesome movies he had seen on the subject. When an arm fell across Michael's leg, he looked down into the eyes of the soldier who had collapsed and realized the soldier was even younger than he—and, now, would never be any older.

Michael stared into the dead boy's face until Chamberlain's hand broke his trance. The man gently brushed the young soldier's eyes, closing them, and said, "Neilson. He was a good kid." He gestured to a man, obviously dead, lying across the rock wall no more than ten yards away. "That was his father. Both joined when this regiment was formed last fall. There were a thousand of us then. The three hundred that're left are strung out along this pile of rocks."

Chamberlain stood up and offered his hand to Michael. Helping him to his feet, he said, "I'm Colonel Chamberlain. Joshua Lawrence Chamberlain. I know why you're here, but I don't know your name."

"I'm Michael Holder, sir. Is it safe to be standing up?"

"For the moment," Chamberlain replied as he pulled a small twig from his mustache. "But they'll surely be back. That was the fourth time they made a try for us already."

"Who are 'they'?" Michael stammered.

The colonel cocked his head and frowned. "Why, Lee's boys . . . the Army of Northern Virginia. This battle stretches all the way to a little town about a mile that way." Chamberlain pointed with his rifle.

"What's the name of the town?" Michael asked, sensing another history review.

"Gettysburg," Chamberlain offered. "Ever hear of it?"

Michael nodded. "The Civil War," he whispered.

"What?" Chamberlain asked.

"I said this is the Civil War."

"Hmmph," Chamberlain snorted. "That may be what

you call it, but stick around. I can assure you there's nothing civil about it. Come with me," he said, beginning to walk. "We won't have much time." The colonel climbed onto a big rock and helped Michael up beside him. "You can see them from here," he said.

Michael squinted through the smoke that still lay thick in the air. Following Chamberlain's gaze, he saw the gray and pale yellow uniforms of the Confederate army massing below. Michael could see their hats and the occasional face looking up the hill.

"Who are you?" Michael asked.

Chamberlain jerked his head sharply toward his visitor. "What? I told you. My name is—"

"Sorry, that's not what I meant," Michael interrupted. "No offense, but are you famous? The other people I saw were . . . well . . . famous."

Chamberlain laughed dryly. "Famous? Ten months ago, I was a schoolteacher. Now I'm a soldier. For a while, anyway. Actually, it was about the time I joined up that I started dreaming about you. I knew what you looked like, how tall you were." The colonel tugged at Michael's sleeve. "I even knew you'd be wearing this. These dreams were not like any others—strange, constant, every night for months. You want to hear something spooky? Just before you arrived—there in the middle of the fight—I looked up and raised my hand and you appeared. I closed my fist on your shirt and pulled you down. When I raised my hand to grab you, I knew you'd be there. It was just like in my dreams."

"Why are you here?" Michael asked.

Chamberlain eyed him curiously. "Do you mean the war in general or this specific hill?"

"Both, I guess."

"Hmm." Chamberlain stroked his beard. "I joined the Union army for a myriad of reasons—same as everyone else, really. We got caught up in the patriotism. We were bored. We were ashamed *not* to join. We thought it'd be quick and fun. For the most part, though, I think the vast majority of our men left their homes and families because it was the right thing to do."

Chamberlain was interrupted by one of the men forming behind fallen trees. "Colonel!" the man yelled. "The brush is too thick. We can't see thirty yards!"

"Stay where you are, son," Chamberlain yelled back. "They'll be a lot closer than that!"

Chamberlain was silent for a few moments when

Michael prompted him, "Colonel? . . . You said you joined because it was the right thing to do."

"Yes," Chamberlain continued. "Over the centuries, wars have been fought for land or women or money. More than a few times, men have fought because a king or president or someone told them to fight." Chamberlain turned to look Michael squarely in the eye. "Michael Holder, I say to you now that this is the first time in history that men have fought to set another man free. Most of us Maine boys have never even seen black skin on a man, but if it is true that all men are created equal, then we are fighting for each other. We are fighting because it's the right thing to do. And now, I'm just hoping it'll all be worth it."

The colonel picked a nearby weed and stood up. He pointed the weed toward the wall. "This wall won't hold 'em much longer, and we don't have enough men left. I have a feeling," he said, "that if we lose this fight, the war will be over."

Michael stepped up beside the colonel. "Why did you choose this place to defend?"

"I didn't choose it," Chamberlain said dryly. "Colonel Vincent placed me here this morning."

five

"Why did he put you here—out in the middle of nowhere?" Michael pressed.

"We are the extreme left of the Union army. The Eighty-third Pennsylvania is formed on our right, but to our left, nothing. We are the end of a line that runs from here all the way back into Gettysburg. That means I cannot withdraw. If the Confederate army flanks us, if the Rebs overrun us, they'll come in behind our cannons and barricades, and the Army of the Potomac will be forfeited. Eighty thousand men would be caught from the back with no protection. And if there're going to try that, first they'll have to come through me."

At that very second, Michael heard an eerie sound echoing from down the hill. Rising to a high, thin pitch, a thousand voices strained in a long, continuous scream. It was the Rebel yell. They were coming! Michael caught glimpses of the soldiers through the trees as they ran up the steep hill.

Chamberlain had just turned to direct Michael off the rock when the cannon shell hit. It struck the base of the rock and threw both men into the air. As Michael hit the ground, he felt like a giant vacuum had sucked all the air from his body. Before he could check to see if he'd been injured—before he could even breathe—Chamberlain had him by the arm, dragging him to the protection of the wall.

Only the cannons were firing now, Michael realized as he tried to get his lungs working again. He could still hear the bloodcurdling yells of the Rebels working their way up the hill. He rolled over onto his knees and glanced over the wall. They were within sight. It seemed to Michael that the Confederate army was about to step into his lap. *Shoot!* he thought. *They're right here! Shoot!*

It felt like an eternity, but finally, Michael heard Chamberlain call out the order, "Hit 'em!" A long, rolling crack of rifle fire rang out. It began near Michael and ran like a fuse up the line to the right. Scores of Rebels fell on the first volley. The Rebels were more careful after that, using trees to shield them from the deadly fire, but still they came.

Chamberlain was directing his men and had moved some distance from Michael. A few of the Rebels had reached the wall now, and most of the shooting was point-blank. The colonel had drawn his pistol, and continued to fire at targets all around him until, without warning, the Rebels pulled back.

As suddenly as they had appeared, they withdrew. Chamberlain's men cautiously stood up and took a look around. Michael walked quickly to the colonel, who was walking away from him. The rock wall was draped with the bodies of blue and gray. He passed a man who was crying and cursing as he held a younger man in his arms.

Jogging to catch up with Chamberlain, Michael reached out and touched his shoulder. "Colonel?" he said. Chamberlain stopped, staring straight ahead. "Colonel? I know you are very busy, and I don't want to bother you, but why am I here?"

Chamberlain slowly shook his head. "I don't know. I only knew that you would come."

"There is something I should learn from you," Michael pleaded. "Think—what could it be?"

The colonel smiled slightly and raised his eyebrows. "I am fairly certain I have nothing you would care to learn. I am a teacher with a cause in my heart and men to lead. These poor men . . . their leader has no real knowledge of warfare or tactics. I am only a stubborn man. That is my greatest advantage in this fight. I have deep within me the inability to do nothing. I may die today, but I will not die with a bullet in my back. I will *not* die in retreat. I am, at least, like the apostle Paul, who wrote, 'This one thing I do . . . I press toward the mark.'"

"Do you have a note to give me?" Michael asked.

For a second, Michael could see that Chamberlain did not understand his question. Then recognition flared in his eyes. "Yes," he said. "I do. I had almost forgotten."

Digging into his pocket, he pulled out a small pouch. The pouch was hand-sized, navy blue, with two crossed swords, the symbol of a fighting man, embroidered on the flap. It had been sewn from stout cloth, but the rough treatment it had received had worn the pouch to a moleskin softness. The two gold buttons that closed the flap were metal, engraved with the image of an eagle. The pouch was beaten and threadbare, but it was still handsome—regal in a sense—the possession of an officer.

Chamberlain opened the pouch and pulled out a small, folded piece of paper. "I wrote this more than two months ago," he said. Passing the paper to Michael, he said, "I'm a little foggy on what I actually wrote. I woke up in the middle of the night after one of those dreams. The words you have there were rumbling around in my head as plain as day. I lit the lamp, found an inkwell, and put them to paper. I knew they were for you."

"Thank you," Michael said, taking the paper in his hand.

"My pleasure," Chamberlain replied. "All of this has been a very curious situation. By the way, how do you get out of here?"

Michael held up the paper. "All I have to do is read this—" he snapped his fingers, "—and I'm gone."

Chamberlain looked around him. Noticing several men approaching, he put his hand on Michael's shoulder, squeezed it, and said, "If that's all you have to do, then, brother, you might want to read it now."

He began to leave, then looked back at Michael. Still in his hand was the small, canvas pouch. Holding it out, he offered it to Michael. Wordlessly, Michael took the gift and watched the colonel walk away. Everything in him wanted to take Chamberlain's advice. *Read the paper now*, he told himself. *Get out of here.* But something kept nudging him to stay, to watch.

After placing the piece of paper back into the pouch, Michael shoved the whole thing in his jeans pocket and eased up to the group of men surrounding Colonel Chamberlain.

"Tozier!" Chamberlain called to a soldier who had a thick wad of torn cloth stuck into a hole in his shoulder where he had been wounded earlier while carrying the battle flag.

"No help from the Eighty-third," Tozier growled. "They're shot to ribbons. All they can do is extend the line a bit . . . and we're getting murdered on the flank."

"Can we extend?" Chamberlain asked.

"There's nothing to extend, sir," another man answered. "Over half our men are down."

"How are we for ammunition?"

"We've been shooting a lot."

"I know we've been shooting a lot! I want to know how we're holding out."

"I'll check, sir."

As the man moved off, a voice came from a young soldier who had climbed a tree. "They're forming again, Colonel." Chamberlain looked up to see the boy pointing downhill. "They're forming up right now," he said, "and they've been reinforced. There's more of them this time."

"Sir!" An officer, out of breath, stumbled into their midst. "Colonel Chamberlain, sir. Sir . . . Colonel Vincent is dead."

"Are you sure, Thomas?"

"Yes, sir. He was shot right at the first of the fight. We were firmed up by Weed's Brigade in the front, but now Weed is dead. They moved Hazlett's Battery up top. Hazlett's dead too."

five

The soldier who had gone to check ammunition came running back. "Sir," he began, "we're out. One, two rounds per man at the most. Some of the men have nothing at all."

Chamberlain turned to a thin man standing to his right. "Spear," he said calmly, "tell the boys to take ammunition from the wounded and dead."

"Maybe we should think about pulling out, sir," Spear said cautiously.

"We will *not* be pulling out, Sergeant," Chamberlain replied grimly. "Carry out my orders, please."

"Colonel," Tozier spoke up. "Sir, we won't hold 'em again. You know we won't."

"Sir," the boy called from the tree, "here they come."

Michael had been listening to the exchange between the officers, fascinated by the horror of their situation, but when he heard the Rebel yells coursing up through the trees once more, his blood turned icy cold. *I've waited too late to read the paper,* he thought. *I'll never get out of here now.* As he grabbed for the pouch, a calm washed over him, and he felt the same urge—wait, watch, listen, learn.

Chamberlain was standing in full view on top of the wall, his arms crossed, staring down at the advancing enemy. Sergeant Spear had returned and was standing at the colonel's feet. Tozier and two other men were bunched below. Michael stood several feet behind the group. "Sir!" Tozier shouted. "Give an order!"

Chamberlain remained stoic. He walked away from the group of men, and Michael heard him speaking softly, in a firm, resolved voice. "We can't retreat," he said to himself. "We can't stay here. When I am faced with the choice of doing nothing or doing something, I will always choose to act. I am a person of action." Turning his back to the Rebels, he looked down at his men. "Fix bayonets," he called.

At first, no one moved. They simply stared at him with open mouths. "We'll have the advantage of moving downhill," Chamberlain said. "Fix bayonets now. Execute a great right wheel of the entire regiment. Swing the left first."

"Sir, wait—what's a great right wheel?" one of the officers yelled. But the colonel had already jumped from the rocks.

Tozier answered the question. "He means to charge, Melcher. A 'great right wheel' is an all-out charge."

Michael watched in awe as Chamberlain drew his sword, leaped up onto the wall again, and shouted, "Bayonets! Bayonets!" Turning, the colonel pointed the sword directly at Michael and slightly bowed his head. Then with a power born of righteousness and fear, the schoolteacher from Maine roared, "Charge! Charge! Charge!" to his men. And they did.

Tumbling over the wall, the men who were left raised their voices to meet the voice of their leader. "Charge!" they cried. "Charge! Charge!"

Michael rushed to the wall and looked downhill. He was stunned to see the advancing Confederate force stop in its tracks. Almost immediately, the Rebels turned and ran. A few of the braver souls emptied their rifles before dropping them to follow the rest. About seventy yards down the slope, Michael caught sight of Chamberlain. He had his left hand on the trunk of a tree, and in his right, he held the sword, the point of which was resting on the collarbone of a Rebel officer. The man had his hands up. It was over.

Michael climbed over the rocks and sat down. With his back to the wall, he pulled the pouch from his pocket. As he looked down the slope, Michael brushed his fingers over the silky smoothness of the material. Unbuttoning the flap, Michael removed the paper that Chamberlain had written. After taking a final glance downhill and a deep breath, Michael unfolded the paper.

The Third Decision for Success

I am a person of action.

Beginning today, I will create a new future by creating a new me. No longer will I dwell in a pit of despair, moaning over squandered time and lost opportunity. I can do nothing about the past. My future is immediate. I will grasp it with both hands and carry it with running feet. I will seize this moment. I choose now.

I am a person of action. I am energetic. I move quickly.

Knowing that laziness is a sin, I will create a habit of lively behavior. I will walk with a spring in my step and a smile on my face. Wealth and success hide from the sluggard, but rich rewards come to the person who moves quickly.

I am a person of action. I inspire others with my activity. I am a leader.

Leading is doing. To lead, I must move forward. Many people move out of the way for a person on the run; others are caught up in his wake. My activity will create a wave of success for the people who follow. My activity will be consistent. This will instill confidence in my leadership. As a leader, I have the ability to encourage and inspire others to greatness. It is true: an army of sheep led by a lion would defeat an army of lions led by a sheep!

I am a person of action. I can make a decision. I can make it now.

God has given me a healthy mind to gather and sort information and the courage to come to a conclusion. I am not a quivering dog, indecisive and fearful.

I am a person of action. I am daring. I am courageous.

Fear no longer has a place in my life. For too long, fear has outweighed my desire to go for the things I really want. Never again! I have exposed my fear as a vapor, an impostor that never had any power over me in the first place! I do not fear opinion, gossip, or the idle chatter of monkeys, for all are the same to me. I do not fear failure, for in my life, failure is a myth. Failure exists only for the person who quits. I do not quit.

I am courageous. I am a leader. I seize this moment. I choose now.

I am a person of action.

six

The nausea was much stronger this time. When the rock wall disappeared behind Michael's back, he immediately felt a swaying sensation drawing him down, back up, and then down again. He balled his fists, ducked his head, and wondered when the time shift would be over. The sickness was almost overwhelming. Carefully, Michael opened his eyes and immediately understood. The movement was not part of the travel; he had arrived at his destination in less than an instant. He was on a boat.

six

It was dark, but despite the darkness, Michael could see the water in the starlight. The salty smell from summer vacations past told him that he was on the ocean. As his sight adjusted to his surroundings, the motion bothered him less. Feeling around, he found that he was sitting on a large pile of coiled rope. Well, he thought it was rope. It was rougher and less uniform than any rope he'd ever used. It felt like it was made out of grass.

Michael suddenly remembered that he still held Chamberlain's paper in one hand and the pouch in the other. Excited and somewhat amazed that the pouch had come with him, Michael hurriedly placed the paper in the pouch and buttoned it. Then he remembered the page from Truman and King Solomon's leather scroll. Removing them from his pocket, Michael placed the first two priceless notes inside the colonel's pouch with the third and shoved it back into his jeans pocket.

Carefully, Michael rose. He was stiff and somewhat sore as if he'd been still for a long time. Looking up, Michael saw a massive broadcloth—a sail—and smiled. He had sailed with his father some on the lake, but not with a sail this huge! "Dad would really get a kick out of this," he said aloud.

Suddenly, Michael felt very alone and very tired. Sinking down into the pile of rope, he laid his head back as the tears welled up in his eyes. How was his dad? Would he ever see him again? Or his mom? Was she worried about him? Had ten minutes passed . . . or a hundred years?

"My friend! Pssst! My friend!" Michael felt a tugging on his sleeve and opened his eyes. It was still dark, but he felt like he'd been sleeping forever. "My friend," a figure hissed urgently, "please, if you will, come with me." After being practically jerked to his feet, Michael followed the outline of a small, stocky man as he lightly stepped around barrels, ropes, and poles, working his way to the center of the boat.

Trying to keep up, Michael almost tripped several times, until, finally, the man stopped at the base of the mast. The large pole, bigger around than Michael could have reached, rose up into the darkness. Supporting the mainsail, it was covered in ropes and buckles. Without a glance at Michael, the man said simply, "Up," and motioned with his hand for Michael to follow.

The man climbed so fast that he was almost out of sight in seconds. Michael hurried to keep up, but it was like crawling through a spider's web. In only a short time, however, he felt a hand grasp the back of his shirt. The small man was very strong. He heaved Michael up, over the lip, and into a wooden cup built around the top of the mast. They were in the crow's nest.

The man smoothed Michael's shirt where he had grabbed it, then placed both hands on Michael's shoulders. "Welcome. Welcome, my friend," he said quietly, but with enthusiasm. "I am most honored to make your acquaintance. And your name is . . . ?"

"My name is Michael, Michael Holder."

"Ah, Señor Holder. May I call you Michael?"

"Yes, of course."

"Excellent! Are you hungry?"

"No, not really. I—"

"Good! We have very little to eat, and what we *do* have contains wee bugs!" Michael winced. "But there is no problem," the man said. "You will see. Our journey is almost at an end."

Despite the darkness, the reflection of the stars from the water illuminated the crow's nest in a soft glow. Michael could see the man clearly now. He had reddish-brown hair, very curly, that fell almost to his shoulders. A triangular, green felt hat was set far back on his head, the forward point jutting toward the sky. The rest of his clothes, except for a stout canvas jacket, were in tatters. The man's pants fell in strips around his ankles, and his shoes were virtually nonexistent—hard leather wrapped around his feet.

"What's *your* name, sir?" Michael asked.

"Why, yes, of course." The man put a hand to his head. "How rude of me! I am Capitán Colón. Capitán Cristóbal Colón, master of the *Santa Maria*, at your service." He gave a little bow.

"*Santa Maria?* Colón?" Michael asked. "Columbus? You are Christopher Columbus?"

"Yes." The man smiled, a bit confused. "Columbus is the English pronunciation of my name, but your Portuguese is flawless. I naturally assumed . . ."

Michael grinned. "I'm speaking Portuguese tonight only."

Columbus tilted his head as if he were trying to see what Michael thought was humorous. "I see," he said, though, clearly, he did not. Clapping his hands and rubbing them together, Columbus changed the subject. "Whatever it is that you are doing tonight," he said, "the night itself will soon be over. The sun will join us shortly!"

The rocking of the vessel seemed more intense in the

high perch, but otherwise, Michael felt safe, almost comfortable. Looking behind the *Santa Maria*, he could just make out the shadows of two other boats.

"The *Niña* and the *Pinta?*" Michael asked, proud of himself for remembering the names from his studies of Christopher Columbus.

"Why, yes," Columbus answered. "Seaworthy vessels both, though not quite so luxurious as this." He flung his arms out below him toward the deck of the *Santa Maria*.

Michael tried not to smile. "Do you know where you are?" he asked.

"Certainly." Columbus smiled. "I am right here! Do you know where *you* are?"

Michael looked around. "The Atlantic Ocean?"

"Good! Good!" Columbus said, clapping Michael on the back. "You are a wonderful navigator!"

Michael was a little uneasy. "Do you *really* not know where you are?"

"Does that have any bearing on what I can accomplish?" Columbus asked in return.

"Um, I don't quite understand," Michael said.

"I have heard that question in one form or another since I was a child," Columbus began. "Do you know where you are? Do you know *what* you are? Colón, you are uneducated. Colón, you are poor. You are the son of a weaver! What do you know about the sea?" He shook his head in disgust. "'Do you know where you are?' is a question that interests me not in the least! Now, 'Do you know where you are going?'—there is a question I can answer! So, ask me that."

"Excuse me? Ask you . . . ?"

"Ask me, 'Do you know where you are going?' Ask me!"

"Okay." Michael shrugged. "Do you know where you are going?"

For the few minutes they had been in the crow's nest, they had conversed in rather quiet, measured tones. At that point, however, Columbus received the question he had been waiting for. He boomed out the answer. Carrying across the water, it sounded like the voice of God Himself. Throwing his hand forward, pointing into the western sky, he cried, "Yes! Yes! I *know* where I am going! I am going to a new world!"

Shivers ran up Michael's spine as he watched the great explorer point into the darkness. For a moment, neither of them said a word. Clearing his throat, Michael broke the silence. "How long since you left Spain?" he asked.

"Sixty-four days," Columbus said, lowering his arm, "and today we shall see land. Look behind us." Michael turned and saw a brightening in the eastern sky. "Dawn will be breaking soon. When it does, directly in front of the *Santa Maria* will be land. Beautiful land with trees and fruit and animals and people who will welcome us as heroes! The water gushing from the ground will be cold and pure. It will sparkle as if sprinkled with diamonds! This will be a place for men's dreams to come true—a glorious new world claimed by Cristóbal Colón in the name of King Ferdinand and Queen Isabella!"

Michael leaned forward. "They're the king and queen of Spain, right?"

Columbus nodded. "They are the financiers of this expedition. King John of Portugal, *my* king, said no to this grand opportunity, as did the kings and queens of many other countries. It took nineteen years to find sponsorship. For nineteen years, I endured the agony of public humiliation for my convictions."

"What convictions?" Michael asked.

"The conviction . . . ," Columbus said, his voice rising, "no, the absolute certainty that I can establish a new trade route by sailing west. West!"

Columbus grabbed Michael by the shoulders and shook him once as he said, "My friend! The world is a sphere! It is not flat! We are sailing *around* the earth on the smooth surface of a sphere. We will not fall off some imaginary edge!"

"And you are the only person who believes that?" Michael asked.

"At this moment, yes," Columbus admitted, "but that bothers me not in the least. Truth is truth. If a thousand people believe something foolish, it is still foolish! Truth is never dependent upon consensus of opinion."

"But don't you care that people think you are . . . well, you know . . . crazy?"

"My friend," Columbus said with a smile, "if you worry about what other people think of you, then you will have more confidence in their opinion than you have in your own. Poor is the man whose future depends on the opinions and permission of others."

"But how—"

Columbus put his hand out to silence him. "Please, my friend," he said, "quiet for a time." Michael did as he asked and followed his gaze into the western sky. The sun was just beginning to rise, creating miles of a glimmering ocean. Columbus peered ahead and for one full minute, he didn't move. Two minutes . . . and then ten. Only his eyes shifted as he scanned the line where the water touched the sky. After almost half an hour, Columbus straightened his back and rubbed his eyes.

"Nothing?" Michael whispered.

"Yes, something," Columbus answered.

Michael looked around. "You see land?"

"Yes," the great man said simply.

Michael frowned. He still couldn't see it. "Point it out to me, would you?"

"Señor Holder," Columbus began, "you are looking in the wrong direction. Today you will not see land off the bow of my ship. You will see land only by looking into my eyes."

Michael felt like he'd been tricked. "So there's no land?"

"Yes, there is land," Columbus replied, "and it is right there." He pointed past the bow of the ship. I see it as plainly as I see you." Columbus was silent as he gazed into the water.

For a brief time, Michael didn't breathe. His eyes were fixed on the man before him. *What could I accomplish,* Michael wondered, *with a spirit as powerful as this?*

Columbus inhaled deeply and turned to Michael. "Most people fail at whatever they attempt because of an undecided heart. Should I? Should I not? Go forward? Go back? Success requires a committed heart. When challenged, the committed heart will search for a solution. The undecided heart searches for an escape."

Columbus cleared his throat, coughing gently, then continued, "A committed heart does not wait for conditions to be exactly right. Why? Because conditions are *never* exactly right. Indecision limits the Almighty and His ability to perform miracles in your life. If He has put the vision in you, proceed! To wait, to wonder, to doubt, to be indecisive about that vision is to disobey God."

Without taking his eyes off the water, Columbus reached under his jacket and removed a parchment. "For you," he said. Unfolding it, he handed it to Michael.

Michael took the yellowed paper, glanced at it briefly, and said, "You *will* find your new world."

Columbus, eyes still straight ahead, spoke quietly, "Yes, I know."

Michael smiled and shook his head in wonder. "*How* do you know?"

Columbus turned and looked at Michael. "I have a decided heart," he said and turned back.

Stealing one last glance at the man who had penned the words, Michael began to read.

The Fourth Decision for Success

I have a decided heart.

A wise man once said, "A journey of a thousand miles begins with a single step." Knowing this to be true, I am taking my first step today. For too long my feet have been tentative, shuffling left and right, more backward than forward as my heart gauged the direction of the wind. The power to control direction belongs to me. Today I will begin to exercise that power. My course has been charted.

I have a decided heart. I am passionate about my vision for the future.

I will wake every morning with an excitement about the new day and the opportunity it holds. My thoughts and actions will work in a forward motion, never sliding into the dark forest of doubt or the muddy quicksand of self-pity. I will freely give my vision for the future to others, and as they see the belief in my eyes, they will follow me.

I will lay my head on my pillow at night happily exhausted, knowing that I have done everything within my power to move the mountains in my path. As I sleep, the same dream that dominates my waking hours will be with me in the dark. Yes, I have a dream. It is a great dream, and I will never apologize for it. Neither will I ever let it go, for if I did, my life would be finished. A person without a dream never had a dream come true.

I have a decided heart. I will not wait.

What I put off until tomorrow, I will put off until the next day as well. I do not procrastinate. All my problems become smaller when I confront them. If I touch a thistle with caution, it will prick me, but if I grasp it boldly, its spines crumble into dust.

I will not wait. I am passionate about my vision for the future. My course has already been charted. My destiny is assured.

I have a decided heart.

seven

Michael felt the swaying of the *Santa Maria* as he looked up from the parchment. He stood up and saw that he was no longer in the crow's nest, but his feet seemed to be planted firmly in midair, moving at an ever-increasing pace away from the ship.

In the next instant, Michael was standing in a small room. The air was musty, and the only light in the room came from a bare bulb hanging on a wire from the ceiling. Michael counted seven people in the room with him. Incredibly, they were motionless. A man and a woman were seated at a tiny table. Two teenagers, a boy and a girl, were on the floor, an interrupted card game between them, and the rest, two men and a woman, appeared to have stopped in midstride. Each person wore a look of terror.

Michael heard knocking on the wall behind him and the muffled voices of men. As looked toward the sound, he noticed a small girl he had missed before. She was thin and sharply featured with dark wavy hair and eyes so black that they shined. She appeared to be twelve or thirteen and wore a faded, blue cotton dress that seemed at home in the dingy room.

She was standing so close to Michael that he had literally looked over her. This girl, too, was not moving, but as he caught her gaze, she slowly raised a finger to her lips.

After what seemed an eternity, the noise ceased. There was no more knocking, no voices, just the tense silence of the room. And still, no one moved. Finally, the man at the table took a deep breath and blew it out with a whoosh. "It is all right now, everyone," he said quietly. And with that, the people in the room shook their heads and softly began talking to each other.

"This was close," said the teenage boy on the floor. "If there had been dogs . . ."

A tall woman, her hair rolled tightly into a bun, began weeping softly. "Now then, Petronella," her husband said as he put his arms around her. "We are safe. Shhh, hush now." He turned to the boy and said sternly, "Peter, that'll be enough about what might have been. You've upset your mother and most everyone else, I expect. We'll have no more about dogs."

"I was just saying—" Peter began.

"Yes," the man interrupted, "and I was just saying that will be enough!"

Michael watched as the man led his wife into a narrow room to his left. Before the door closed, he saw a mattress on the floor and a stack of magazines. The young girl gently guided Michael to a corner and whispered, "Stay here for now, but when I leave the room, follow me."

She moved toward the couple sitting at the table. The man looked tired, and his clothes were worn, but he was clean-shaven except for a small mustache. Michael thought him a rather distinguished sort. The woman sitting across from him was ghostly pale, as if she'd recently been ill. Nevertheless, she smiled as the girl approached.

"Papa," the girl said. "May I go upstairs?"

The man smiled. "Time to be alone again, is it, Anne?"

"Yes, Papa."

"Then certainly you may go," he said. She glanced at Michael and moved to a stairway at the back of the room. Without a sound, she went up the staircase and out of sight.

Michael followed quickly, dodging the other people in the room as he passed. As he came up the stairs, he saw the girl motioning for him to hurry. The staircase seemed to go directly to the ceiling, but as Michael soon saw, there was a hatch cover that provided entrance to the attic.

As soon as they were inside, the girl replaced the cover and said, "I am so excited to meet you that I almost cannot breathe!" She clapped her hands together quickly, but softly. "This is thrilling, is it not?"

"Yes." Michael grinned at her enthusiasm. Looking around he saw that there was not a stick of furniture or a box of anything stored in the attic—just dust and dirt.

"I expected you, did you know?" she said. "A dream is how. I even know your name. It is Michael Holder. I wrote you a note just this morning. Should I get it now?"

"No, no," Michael chuckled. "Hang on a minute. I don't even know where I am."

"Why, you are in Amsterdam," the girl said. She took

Michael's hand and pulled him toward a window. "Come," she said with a little smile, "I will show you the city." She got down on her hands and knees. "It's all right to peek from the corner. You too! Come now!"

Michael got down on his hands and knees and crawled to the edge of the window where she was waiting underneath the sill. As he settled himself into a more comfortable position, he said, "I heard your father call you Anne."

"Yes," she replied. "And my sister's name is Margo. She is very quiet. She was the one playing cards with the boy downstairs. His name is Peter. Peter Van Daan."

"What is your last name?" Michael asked.

"Frank," she answered. "My papa's name is Otto, and Edith is my mother. Peter's parents are Mr. Herman and Mrs. Petronella. She was the one who cried, but of course, she always cries. . . ."

Michael didn't know how long Anne talked. He wasn't really listening anyway. *Anne Frank,* he thought. *Anne Frank! This is the girl whose diary I read in English last year! I am in the annex!* The annex, he knew, was several secret rooms connected to the back of a warehouse.

" . . . Don't you think?" Anne said as she looked directly at Michael, obviously expecting a response.

Michael was caught off guard by the pause in her non-stop chatter. "I'm sorry. What?"

"I said," Anne answered slowly, "that Peter is very handsome, don't you think?"

"Peter?" Michael thought for a moment. "Oh, the boy downstairs, yes. Yes, he is!" Trying to change the subject, Michael asked, "How long have you been here?"

"One year and four months," she said quickly.

"Do you know today's date?"

"Certainly. Today is Thursday, October 28, 1943. We went into hiding last year on the first Sunday in July, the fifth it was." Anne glanced up at the window. "None of us has been outside in a very long time."

"How do you get food in here?"

"Miep."

"Who is . . . ?"

"Miep is Papa's secretary. She still comes to work in the warehouse every day. After hours, she and her husband, Henk, move the bookcase in the accounting room and come through the door behind it."

"Anne," Michael began, "when I arrived—"

"Oh, yes," Anne broke in. "You appeared directly in front of me! Have you done that before? Does it hurt?"

Michael smiled in spite of the interruption. He could understand her excitement. A new person to talk to must be thrilling after sixteen months. "Yes, I have done it before, and no, it doesn't hurt." Michael tried again to ask his question. "Anne, who was knocking on the walls?"

"Nazi soldiers," Anne said. "Papa calls them Gestapo. He says they dress in black. They have come now two times. We are quiet, and they go away." She turned and got up on her knees, rising carefully to put one eye in the corner of the window. "If you do this, you can see most of Amsterdam."

Michael looked out the opposite corner. To his left, he saw a huge chestnut tree, and across the street, a clock tower stood like the centerpiece of the city.

"That's the Westerkerk," Anne said. "I can lie here and watch the hands move." Anne lay down flat on the floor.

He watched the little girl staring up at the gigantic clock. "What are you thinking?" he asked.

"About the clock," Anne said. "Sometimes I wish for it to speed up, and at other times I beg it to slow down. But it never hears me. It is always the same."

Michael was startled by the sound of whistles and loud, angry voices shattering the silence of the street below them. "What is that?" Michael asked.

"It's a razia," Anne answered with no emotion. "They are rounding up Jews. It makes me wonder about my friends. I don't know what has happened to any of them." For several moments, she was quiet, thoughtful. Michael said nothing. Then she looked directly at him and said, "Everyone is being taken away to camps. Did you know? The Germans say that the Jews are working and living comfortably there, but it is not true."

Michael was careful with his words. "How do you know that?"

Anne shrugged. "We all know. Letters are censored, of course, but occasionally the truth is made known. Miep received a postcard from a friend who had been taken away. It said the food was good and conditions were superb, but at the end of the message, he wrote: 'Give my regards to Ellen de Groot.'" She paused. "The words were Dutch, of course. The German censors did not know that *ellende* means 'misery,' and *groot* is 'terrible.'"

Without warning, the Westerkerk began to chime. Anne placed her hands over her ears and smiled at Michael, who had nearly jumped out of his skin when the chiming began less than seventy feet away.

"It is only a bit too loud," Anne said, giggling at her understatement.

Michael smiled. "How do you sleep with that thing ringing day and night?"

"Actually," Anne said, "we don't even notice it much anymore. Mrs. Petronella is the only one of us who even comments. Papa says the clock is a good thing for her because it provides something to complain about every hour on the hour!"

Michael laughed. "What about you?" he asked. "What do you complain about?"

"I do not complain," Anne said. "Papa says complaining is an activity just as jumping rope or listening to the radio is an activity. One may choose to turn on the radio. One may choose to complain, and one may choose not to complain. I choose not to complain."

Michael stared at the sincere little girl for a moment, then said, "No offense, but have you taken a look around here? These are pretty rough conditions for anyone, never mind a girl your age. How can you *not* complain?"

Anne looked a bit confused, and then answered patiently, "Our lives are shaped by choice, Michael. First, we make choices. Then our choices make us." She took a deep breath. "Yes, an ungrateful person might see a place that is too small for eight people, a diet that is limited and portions that are too meager, or only three dresses for two girls to share. But gratefulness is also a choice. I see an annex that hides eight people while others are being herded onto railway cars. I see food that is generously provided by Miep, whose family uses their ration cards for us. I see an extra dress for my sister and me while there are surely those who have nothing. I choose to be grateful. I choose not to complain."

Michael was amazed. He thought of his room full of stuff at home, his closet full of clothes, the car he had carelessly wrecked. He tucked one leg under the other, sitting cross-legged, and shook his head as if to clear the cobwebs. "Are you honestly telling me that you are always in a good mood?"

Anne had folded her legs to mimic the way Michael was sitting. As she draped her dress over her knees, she laughed. "Of course not, silly! But if I ever find myself in a bad mood, I immediately make a choice to be happy. In fact, that is the first choice I make every day. I say out loud to my mirror, 'Today, I will choose to be happy!' I smile into the mirror and laugh even if I am sad. I just say, 'Ha, ha, ha, ha!' And soon, I am happy, exactly as I have chosen to be."

Michael was shaking his head in wonder. "You are a special girl, Anne."

"Thank you," she said. "That is also a choice."

Michael leaned forward. "Really," he said with his eyebrows raised. "How is that?"

"My life—my personality, my habits, even my speech—is a combination of the books I choose to read, the people I choose to listen to, and the thoughts I choose to tolerate in my mind. Before the war, when I was a little girl, my papa took me to the park to hear the orchestra play. At the end of the concert, from behind the musicians, a hundred helium balloons of red and blue and yellow and green floated up into the sky. It was so exciting!

"I tugged on Papa's arm and asked, 'Papa, which color balloon will go the highest?' And he said to me, 'Anne, it's not the color of the balloon that's important. It's what's inside that makes all the difference.'"

For a moment, Anne was quiet. Then she looked Michael directly in the eye, lifted her chin, and said, "You know, I don't believe that being Jewish or Aryan or African has any bearing on what one can become. Greatness does not care if one is a girl or a boy. If it's what's inside that makes all the difference, then the difference is made when we choose what goes inside."

Anne looked toward the clock again. Michael hadn't noticed the darkness that had filled the attic, but now he realized that only the glow of the light from the Westerkerk enabled him to see Anne's face. "I must get ready for dinner soon," she said. "Come with me to my room. I have written something for you."

Michael followed Anne through the hatch in the attic, down the stairs, and back into the living area. "Dinner is almost on the table, dear," her mother said as the two walked by. "Five minutes. No longer."

"Yes, Mother," she answered as she led Michael to a door to the right of the staircase. They walked into a room no larger than a closet. A small mattress lay on the floor with two stacks of books beside the only pillow. "Margo and I share this room," Anne said. "It is very close, but we respect each other's privacy."

Michael didn't see *any* room for privacy. Above the bed were pictures from magazines and newspapers that had been glued to the wall. "Are these yours?" Michael asked.

"Yes," Anne smiled. "Beautiful, aren't they?"

Michael looked more closely. There were pictures of old

movie stars, and a picture of a statue by Michelangelo was positioned over a picture of a house in the country. To the left was a black-and-white photo of a rose that someone had colored pink. Spread all over the wall were pictures of cute, cuddly babies. "Yes, they are beautiful," Michael answered. "What are they for?"

"My future," Anne whispered softly as she reached out to touch the picture of the rose. "These are the people I want to meet, the places I want to see, and the things I want in my life. Laughter and love and a home with a husband, maybe Peter, and lots of babies." Suddenly tears came to her eyes. "Michael, if it were you here, instead of me, would you be afraid?"

Michael took a breath and answered, "Yes, I think I would be afraid, Anne. Are you?"

Anne pulled her hand down from the rose and clasped both hands in front of her. She cut her eyes toward Michael, and then looked back at the pictures. "Sometimes," she said. "But most often, I choose not to be. Papa says, 'Fear is a poor chisel with which to carve out tomorrow.'"

Turning, she continued, "I will have a tomorrow, Michael. Margo and Mrs. Petronella, they make fun of me. They say I live in a dream world, that I do not face reality. This is not true. I know that the war is horrible. I understand that we are in terrible danger here. I do not deny the reality of our situation. I deny the finality of it. This, too, shall pass."

Anne knelt down and reached under the mattress. She pulled out a red and orange checkered, clothbound book. "This is my diary," she said. "Papa gave it to me for my birthday, June twelfth." She thumbed through quickly until she found what she was looking for. "These are yours," she said and carefully tore several pages from the small journal.

Michael took the pages from her hand and watched as she placed what he knew to be her life's work back under the dirty mattress. "Thank you, Anne."

She stood awkwardly in front of him for a minute. "I must go eat," she said. "You will be gone when I return?"

"Yes."

"Then remember me," Anne said, smiling. "I will remember you. But most of all, we both must remember that life itself is a privilege, but to live life to its fullest—well, that is a choice!"

And with that, she hugged Michael and quickly left the room, closing the door behind her. Michael sat down on the mattress and began to read—four small pages, written with a pencil, in the handwriting of a young girl.

The Fifth Decision for Success

Today I will choose to be happy.

From this very moment, I am a happy person, for I now truly understand the meaning of happiness. Few others before me have been able to grasp the truth that enables one to live happily every day. I now know that happiness is not some unattainable fairy tale floating just out of my reach. Happiness is a choice. Happiness is the end result of certain thoughts and activities.

Today I will choose to be happy. I will greet each day with laughter.

When I wake in the morning, I will laugh out loud. And with that laugh, excitement will begin to flow through my bloodstream. I will feel differently. I will be different! I will be open to the possibilities of the day. I will be happy!

Laughter is an outward expression of enthusiasm, and I know that enthusiasm fuels the world. I will laugh throughout the day. I will laugh while I am alone, and I will laugh when talking to others. People are drawn to me because I have laughter in my heart. The world belongs to the enthusiastic, for people will follow them anywhere!

Today I will choose to be happy. I will smile at every person I meet.

My smile has become my calling card. It is the most potent weapon I possess. My smile can create bonds, break ice, and calm storms. I will use my smile constantly. I will always smile first. That display of a good attitude will tell others what I expect in return.

Today I will choose to be happy. I have a grateful spirit.

In the past, I have been discouraged until I compared the condition of my life to others less fortunate. Just as a fresh breeze cleans smoke from the air, a grateful spirit removes a dark cloud of despair. The seeds of depression cannot take root in a thankful heart.

God has given me many gifts, and for these I will remember to be grateful. Too many times I have prayed the prayers of a beggar, asking for more and forgetting to give thanks. I do not wish to be seen as a greedy child. I am grateful for sight and sound and breath. If there are ever more blessings than that, I will be grateful for the miracle of abundance.

I will greet each day with laughter. I will smile at every person I meet. I have a grateful spirit.

Today I will choose to be happy.

eight

Michael finished reading the words Anne had written and blinked away a tear beginning to form. He folded the pages, placed them in the pouch, shoved it in his pocket, and stood up. He reached out to touch the picture of the rose Anne had glued to the wall. Touching the bloom, he smiled at the waxy feeling of the pink crayon that had been used to color the black-and-white picture.

Slowly, the rose became blurry. Michael pulled back his hand and wiped his eyes. For a moment, he was a little dizzy, but the feeling quickly passed.

Opening his eyes, he looked at the picture again. It was still blurry but seemed to be clearing. He moved his face only inches from the flower. There! Now it was in focus. The petals even seemed to have depth. Michael reached out with one finger and touched the rose. He gasped. The rose was real.

Michael froze for a moment. He shifted his eyes to see that he was now leaning against an old desk. Easing himself away, he saw that the rose stood in a simple vase on the edge of the desk. Next to the rose sat a pitcher of water and four glasses. Michael stood and looked around. He was in some sort of tent—but not like a tent he'd ever camped in. It was made of white canvas, with dead grass for the floor, and large enough in which to fit three wooden chairs and a desk.

He heard activity outside and moved to the closed flap of the tent. Carefully, he peeked through the opening to see a raised platform about seventy or eighty feet away. A man stood alone behind a podium, speaking to thousands of people. There were saddled horses and carriages and wagons scattered around the crowd. Many had those old-timey umbrellas to ward off the sun and were sitting on quilts on the ground or on top of their wagons.

Michael saw that the tent and stage were on top of a hill surrounded by large trees. Since the trees had lost most of their leaves and the temperature was comfortable, Michael guessed it was fall, and looking at the sun, maybe around noon.

Beyond the crowd, Michael saw fields and forestland that stretched as far as he could see. The area gave him a strange feeling. It seemed eerily familiar, but he couldn't quite place how or why.

Maybe, Michael thought, *the speaker is why I am here.* He turned once again toward the stage and watched the elegantly dressed gentleman. He wore gray pants over polished black boots, and a high white collar rose from the back of a black coat complete with tails. His flowing gray hair completed a look of distinction.

The man also appeared to be quite the speaker. He held the audience's attention by pacing the stage and gesturing dramatically with his hands. Michael couldn't quite hear the speaker's presentation, and then he realized why—there was no microphone or sound system. Because the man faced away from him, Michael could only catch a word here and there.

Several times, the crowd thundered with applause and

once, as the speaker turned, Michael got a clear view of his features. The man was beginning to lose his hair and had a clean-shaven face. His eyebrows were big and bushy; his nose and ears were a bit too large for his head. Michael was a little disappointed. He didn't recognize him at all.

Michael eased away from the tent's door and, contemplating the situation, poured himself a glass of water. *Is that the person I am here to see?* he asked himself, unable to shake the feeling that he was somehow connected to this place.

Suddenly, he heard the sound of horses' hooves and creaking leather saddles just outside the tent. Michael put down his glass and quickly moved to a corner as a man stepped through the flap.

He was a bit older than Michael, about twenty-five, well dressed in a long coat and a high collar. His hair was parted crisply in the middle, and his thin mustache ran in a perfect line above his lips. With the presence of a person who is accustomed to being in charge, the young man walked briskly across the tent directly to the desk. He opened each drawer and inspected the contents before closing it.

Michael saw him pause for a moment when he spied the glass of water. The man picked up the glass and frowned. Shaking his head from side to side with little jerks, he took the glass to the far corner of the tent and poured the water onto the ground. He then placed the empty glass in his coat pocket and moved back to the desk in order to examine the remaining glasses and pitcher. Satisfied, he cautiously looked around the tent and exited.

Michael took a deep breath. Evidently, that was not the person he was there to see. The man hadn't even noticed him standing in plain sight. Before Michael could move, the tent flap opened again.

Stooping low to fit through the opening, a different man entered with his hat under his arm. As the flap closed behind him, the tall man straightened, glanced around, and saw Michael. He smiled and with two quick strides stood before Michael, extending his right hand. "Mr. Holder, isn't it?" the man said with a twinkle in his eye.

Michael's mouth dropped and his knees were wobbly. He wanted to say, "Yes, sir," or "Nice to meet you," or anything, but his throat was so dry that nothing came out. Seeing the confused expression on the gentleman's face and seeing that his hand was still extended, Michael did the only appropriate thing. He shook the hand of Abraham Lincoln.

"I . . . I am honored, sir," Michael managed to stammer.

"The honor is mine, Mr. Holder," the president replied. "After all, it is you who have traveled the greater distance for this occasion. Won't you join me in refreshment?"

Michael nodded and asked, "Sir, where are we?"

Lincoln held up one long finger, and then poured Michael a glass of water. Pouring his own glass, he drank it all, poured another, and sat down. "Bring up a chair," he said as he drew his own from behind the desk.

As Michael sat down, he watched the sixteenth president of the United States cross his legs and loosen his high, starched collar. Michael noticed that the president seemed oversized in all physical respects. His legs, arms, hands, even his face appeared to be too long. Michael smiled as he realized that Abraham Lincoln looked exactly like every picture he'd ever seen of the man. His only surprise was the president's voice. It was not the rich baritone he had imagined, but a higher-pitched voice.

Lincoln placed the glass on the desk and said, "Riding horseback always makes me thirsty, though I'm usually too embarrassed to drink in front of the horse. After all," he chuckled, "I'm not the one who has done all the work!" Michael laughed politely. "So, Mr. Holder, you wish to know where we are."

"Yes, sir, and please, call me Michael."

"Thank you," Lincoln said as he slightly tilted his head toward the young man. "Michael, I am here for two reasons today. First, to dedicate a cemetery. That, by the way, is where we are now . . . Gettysburg, Pennsylvania."

Shivers ran down Michael's spine. "And the date?"

"November 19, 1863."

No wonder this place seems familiar! Michael thought. *I was just here four months ago. Or was it only an hour?* He shook his head to clear his thoughts. "Mr. President, you mentioned two reasons. What's the second?"

Lincoln smiled. "Why, to meet you, of course!" Michael's eyes widened. "You are certainly more important than any remarks I might share with those in attendance today. This cemetery is about the past. You are about the future!"

Michael looked away. "Thanks, but I'm not sure that's exactly right. I'm just hoping there *is* a future. I'm actually going through a horrible time in my life right now."

"Congratulations are in order then! Better days are

most assuredly ahead." The president raised his water glass and exclaimed, "To us, two gentlemen experiencing the worst life has to offer."

Michael wasn't sure whether Lincoln was joking or not. "I'm not kidding," he said slowly.

"Oh, let me assure you," Lincoln said with a tight smile, "neither am I." He reached to his right, across the desk, and picked up his hat. It was the tall, black stovepipe that he wore in every picture that Michael had ever seen of the man. Lincoln let his fingers play softly across the large, silk band. "This is a piece of cloth I carry with me in memory of Willie, my little boy. He died only a few months ago." He sighed. "Now my son Tad has taken to bed . . . deathly ill. And as you might imagine, Mrs. Lincoln did not agree that I should be here today."

"Why did you come?"

"Duty. And the fact that I knew I could choose to pray for my son while wandering about the White House or pray as I pursued the challenge that has been placed before me. I am quite confident the Almighty hears my cry no matter the location."

The president shifted and crossed his arms. "You know, I mentioned that we were two people who were experiencing the worst life has to offer. That is true in a small, selfish way. In a larger sense, however, we are being presented an enormous opportunity for change and the betterment of ourselves."

"Oh, right. 'Personal growth.' You know, I have a teacher at school who is big on that. Most of the kids pretty much tune her out. To be honest, I'm not sure I want any more personal growth anyway," Michael said.

"Of course not!" Lincoln responded. "And wouldn't that be the easy choice to make? It's the most popular choice on the planet! But the question you are facing right now is: how powerful do you want to be?"

Michael tilted his head to the side. "Okay, I'm lost here. What does personal growth have to do with power in the first place? And in the second place, no offense, but I have no interest in power anyway."

Leaning forward, Lincoln said, "Mr. Holder . . . Michael, if that is true, then a great amount of attention is being wasted on you. Some of it at this very moment!"

Michael wasn't sure whether to be insulted or not. He began to speak, "I wasn't the one who—"

Lincoln reached over and touched Michael's knee. Smiling patiently, but interrupting firmly, he said,

"Michael, think with me here. Personal growth leads to power. To do great deeds, great power is essential.

"You see, some people want just enough power to get by. But there are a few of us, Michael, who have latched on to this silly idea that we can change the world. We can ignore what is popular and do what is right."

"Are you ever bothered by what people say about you?" Michael asked.

The president quickly leaned forward with a serious look. "Why? What are they saying?"

Seeing Michael's shocked expression, Lincoln laughed loudly. "I do not worry about what people are saying because if I were to concern myself with the newspaper columns that label me dishonest or stupid, if I had my feelings destroyed every time a political opponent called me an ape or a buffoon, I would never be about the work for which I was born!

"Sooner or later, every man of character will have his character questioned. Every man of honor and courage will be faced with unjust criticism, but never forget that unjust criticism has no impact whatsoever upon the truth. And the only sure way to avoid criticism is to do nothing and be nothing!

"Sometimes we are afraid to step out. We are afraid to become more. But how can we lead others to a destination we have not reached? Keep searching, son. I am urging you to seek the light that to you seems so far in the distance. It will be worth the journey."

At that instant, the door flap was thrown aside, and the young man who had been in the tent earlier entered. Lincoln gestured toward him with his hand and said, "John Hay, my personal secretary."

Michael froze and then held his laughter as the young man hesitated. He watched as Hay looked from side to side, then glanced around the tent and said hesitantly, "Sir?"

Recovering quickly, Lincoln asked, "How may I be of assistance, John?"

Hay wrinkled his brow, puzzled, and continued to peer cautiously behind the president.

"John," Lincoln said again, snapping Hay to attention, "how may I be of assistance?"

"I . . . ahhh . . . excuse the interruption, Mr. President." Now Lincoln stifled a chuckle. "Well . . . sir," Hay stammered, "I wanted you to know that when Mr. Everett has concluded, the Baltimore Glee Club will sing an ode written for this occasion. The music will provide the time necessary to escort you from here to the stage."

"Thank you, John," Lincoln said as he walked toward the opening of the tent. "The beginning of the music, then, will be my cue to join you outside the tent. Until that time, sir, I trust you will maintain my privacy."

The president pulled back the flap to hasten his secretary's departure. Hay ducked through the opening, then turned around, ducked back inside, and asked, "Sir, excuse me, but are you saying that I should not come back inside?"

"That is correct, John."

"So, you will meet me outside the tent when you are ready to go to the stage?"

"Yes, John."

Briefly, Hay paused, his head still sticking into the tent. "Sir, if I may be so bold as to ask—"

"John," Lincoln interrupted.

"Yes, sir?"

"I will meet you outside the tent when I am ready to go to the stage."

"Yes, sir." Hay sighed and slid outside.

The president closed the canvas and, urging Michael to

follow with a jerk of his head, walked quickly to the desk. Tears were streaming down his face as he finally let his laughter burst out.

Gaining control, Lincoln took a deep breath and sighed. "I forgot he could not see you. That was extremely close, my friend."

Michael chuckled. "Yes, it was." He thought for a moment. "What is your part in the ceremony today?"

Lincoln's smile disappeared as he cleared his throat. "Today we take pause from our battles to dedicate one ugly reality of this war: a cemetery. There are quite a few of them around now, as you must know. Certainly more than I can dedicate."

Lincoln frowned and continued, "There were more than fifty thousand casualties here." He was quiet for a moment, and then brightening, he said, "I have General Grant leading the army now. This will not last much longer."

"Are you winning the war?" Michael asked.

"We weren't. I can tell you that! But after this battle, Gettysburg, last July, the outcome seems much brighter indeed."

Michael suddenly had a thought and asked, "Mr.

President, are you familiar with an officer in your army by the name of Colonel Joshua Chamberlain? He is with the Twentieth Maine."

Lincoln cocked his head and thought briefly, then said slowly, "No, I don't believe so. Should I know this man?"

"Maybe. He fought at Gettysburg. When you get back to Washington, you might look him up." The president nodded. "I have another question," Michael continued. "Do you believe that God is on your side?"

Lincoln looked at Michael thoughtfully. "On September twenty-second of last year, I signed a proclamation of emancipation for all slaves specifying that they will be henceforward and forever free. One of my cabinet members made it known to anyone who would listen that a vast majority of the public stood against me and my intention to sign the Emancipation Proclamation. However, my position is that while public opinion may sway back and forth, right and wrong do not.

"So your question was, 'Do I believe that God is on our side?' To be quite honest, I haven't given that question very much attention. I am much more concerned with whether we are on God's side."

Michael remembered something Lincoln had said earlier. "You mentioned Grant," he prompted. "Why will he make such a difference?"

"Because he cares as I do!" came the sharp reply. "Grant wants to win as badly as I do. If you are determined to win, you will have to surround yourself with winners. Don't be discouraged by the people you might choose for your team who talk big but produce little. Grant is the tenth general to lead the Union forces—my tenth try. I just keep putting them in the boat to see who wants to paddle as hard as I do."

"What will you do if . . . when you win?" Michael asked.

"Do you mean, where will I lead this nation?"

"Yes."

"That is a rather easy question to answer. In fact, I have spent many hours in prayerful consideration of my response. The first morning after all hostilities cease, I will greet the day with a forgiving spirit."

Michael was blown away. "How can you? I don't understand!"

"It's a very simple concept actually, and it is the single most important action I take on a regular basis.

Forgiveness allows me to be an effective husband, father, friend, and leader of this country."

Confused, Michael asked, "What does forgiveness have to do with being effective?"

Lincoln thought for a moment, crossed his legs, and responded, "Have you ever been so angry or upset with someone that all you could think of was that person and the horrible way you'd been treated? You think about him when you should be sleeping, and all the things you should have said or would like to say come to mind. When you should be enjoying time with your family or friends, they are no longer foremost in your thoughts. That person who offended you is receiving all your energy. You feel as if you might explode." Leaning forward, he asked, "Have you ever felt this way?"

"Yes." Michael nodded. "I sure have."

Lincoln relaxed back in his chair. "Well, so have I. I owe business failures, marital strife, and defeats in several political races to those very feelings. But I also owe a great deal of the success I enjoy to the discovery of this simple secret."

"What secret?" Michael leaned forward.

"The secret of forgiveness," Lincoln responded. "It is a

secret that is hidden in plain sight. It costs nothing and is worth millions. It is available to everyone and is used by few. If you harness the power of forgiveness, you will be honored, sought after, and, not coincidentally, you will also be forgiven by others!"

Michael looked puzzled. "Well, who am I supposed to forgive?"

"Everyone."

"But what if they don't ask for forgiveness?"

Lincoln raised his dark eyebrows and smiled. "Most will not! Many of these people who occupy our minds with angry thoughts will wander about without any knowledge of our feelings or any conviction that they have done anything wrong!"

Michael frowned. "I'm sure that's all true, but how do you forgive someone who doesn't ask for forgiveness?"

"You know," Lincoln began, "I cannot recall a single book, including the Holy Bible, that says in order for you to forgive someone, he or she has to ask for it. Think about it. The unmistakable truth about forgiveness is that it is not a reward that must be earned; forgiveness is a gift to be given. When I give forgiveness, I free my own spirit to release the anger in my heart. And forgiveness, when granted to others, becomes a gift to myself."

Just then, cheers began outside. The president pulled a pocket watch from his vest and said, "Well, I expect that will be the end of Mr. Everett. Not much longer now."

Michael stood up.

"Sit back down for a moment, son," Lincoln commanded gently, and Michael did.

"Michael, you are at a critical point in your life's race, and there is a person to whom your forgiveness has been withheld. I must warn you that without a forgiving spirit, your effectiveness as a son, a friend, and a man will be at an end. The key to everything your future holds is forgiveness."

Michael's mouth was open, and a look of confusion was written in his eyes. "Who is it?" he said. Lincoln merely looked at him. "Sir? Who is it?"

Lincoln stood up and brushed off the front of his jacket and pants. Michael stood up and said, "Mr. President, you have to tell me who it is!"

The president stepped toward the door. "Listen!" Michael said, putting his hand on Lincoln's arm. "You're about to go out there, and I'll never see you again. You pretty much said that my life would be over if I didn't for-give this person. If it's that important, tell me! Who must I forgive?"

The president looked carefully into Michael's eyes. "Yourself."

Tears formed in Michael's eyes, and he shook his head. "I didn't think . . ."

Lincoln placed his hands on the young man's shoulders. "Michael, your parents are not mad at you. Your teachers are not mad at you. Your friends, of whom I am one, are not mad at you, and God is not mad at you. So, Michael," Lincoln stopped briefly and said with a smile, "don't *you* be mad at you. Forgive yourself. Begin anew."

"Thank you," Michael said as he wiped his eyes on his shirtsleeve.

"I am honored to have been of assistance," Lincoln said. Picking up his hat, he asked, "Would you care to follow me out? You may join the crowd and listen if you wish."

"That would be awesome," Michael said. "By the way, I'm sorry I took up all your prep time here in the tent."

"No problem at all," the president responded. "I've been ready with these remarks for about two weeks."

"Really? You know, when people study you now, or . . . ahh, in the future, one of the things we're taught is that you wrote this speech on the train into Gettysburg."

Lincoln smiled. "No, I wrote the dedication for today back in Washington. But I *was* writing on the train into Gettysburg. In fact, . . ." Lincoln took a piece of paper from inside the band of his stovepipe hat and presented it to Michael. "I was writing this for you."

Michael smiled and followed Lincoln as he began to walk outside. The choir was singing a hymn, and inside the tent, the two men could hear the sounds of twenty thousand people shifting and stretching. Lincoln ducked to go through the opening and then, suddenly, he stopped. With a quizzical expression, he faced Michael and asked, "You say people study me in the future?"

"Yes, sir," Michael answered. .

Lincoln lowered his voice and narrowed his eyes. "Just between you and me, we *do* win this war, correct?"

"Yes, sir."

With a sly smile and one raised eyebrow, he added one last question. "Grant?"

Michael grinned. "Yes, sir," he said and followed the great man out of the tent.

Outside, Michael watched as several men fell in and whisked the president toward the stage. When the choir finished, a man approached the podium and sang out, "Ladies and gentlemen, the president of the United States of America, Abraham Lincoln."

With that, twenty thousand people rose to their feet and cheered. Michael found an empty spot by the stage and looked up at his friend. Then, in a high-pitched, almost shrill voice, Abraham Lincoln spoke the words that would begin the healing of a broken nation:

"Fourscore and seven years ago, our fathers brought forth upon this continent a new nation, conceived in liberty, and dedicated to the proposition that all men are created equal. . . ."

Michael watched in awe and hung on every word of the speech that he had before only skimmed over in his textbook. When the president concluded, the crowd stood quietly for a moment. Then all around him, Michael heard people begin to applaud. Joining them enthusiastically, he watched as Lincoln nodded to the crowd and waved to those farthest from the stage. Looking below him, he caught Michael's gaze and smiled. He then waved to the audience once more, turned, and was gone.

eight

Michael made his way to a large tree away from the crowd. He unfolded the paper given to him by the sixteenth president of the United States and read.

The Sixth Decision for Success

I will greet this day with a forgiving spirit.

For too long, every ounce of forgiveness I owned was locked away, hidden from view, waiting for me to bestow it upon some worthy person. I found most people to be singularly unworthy of my valuable forgiveness, and since they never asked for any, I kept it all for myself. Now, the forgiveness that I hoarded has sprouted inside my heart like a spoiled seed yielding bitter fruit.

No more! At this moment, my life has taken on new hope and assurance. I possess the secret to ridding the heart of anger and resentment. I now understand that forgiveness has value only when it is given away.

I will greet this day with a forgiving spirit. I will forgive even those who do not ask for forgiveness.

Many times, I have seethed in anger at a word or deed thrown into my life by an unthinking or uncaring person. I have wasted valuable hours imagining revenge or confrontation. Now I see the truth revealed about this rock in my shoe. The rage I nurture is often one-sided, for my offender seldom gives thought to his offense!

I will now and forevermore silently offer my forgiveness even to those who do not see that they need it. By the act of forgiving, I am no longer consumed by unproductive thoughts. I give up my bitterness.

I will greet this day with a forgiving spirit. I will forgive those who criticize me unjustly.

Those who are critical of my goals and dreams simply do not understand the higher purpose to which I have been called. I forgive their lack of vision, and I forge ahead. I know that criticism is a part of the price paid for leaping past the average mark.

I will greet this day with a forgiving spirit. I will forgive myself.

For a long time, my greatest enemy has been myself. Every mistake, every stumble I have made has been replayed again and again in my mind. My disappointment in myself has left me paralyzed. When I disappoint myself, I respond with inaction and become more disappointed.

By forgiving myself, I erase the doubts, fears, and frustration that have kept my past in the present. From this day forward, my history will cease to control my destiny. I have forgiven myself. My life has just begun.

I will forgive even those who do not ask for forgiveness. I will forgive those who criticize me unjustly. I will forgive myself.

I will greet this day with a forgiving spirit.

nine

Michael dug the pouch out of his pocket. Carefully, he folded the paper and placed it inside the worn canvas. His hand brushed the smooth skin on which King Solomon had written the Second Decision. "One, two, three, four, five, six." Michael counted the priceless pieces of wisdom aloud. *I'm supposed to receive seven,* he thought. *Where will I go next?*

Michael tensed in expectation of leaping across time and space. But nothing happened. Finally, feelings of weariness from the unbelievable journey overcame Michael.

Unable to keep his eyes open, he put the pouch back in his pocket and lay down. He tried to stay awake and was scared to fall asleep, but he couldn't fight it.

Images of his father lying in the hospital swirled through his mind. "Son, your mother needs you," his father whispered. "Michael, where are you? Are you okay?" his mom pleaded. He tried to reach out to them, but they were just out of his touch. *This is crazy,* Michael thought. *I'm having a dream in the middle of a dream. I have to wake up.* Michael woke in a drenched sweat. He was terrified of closing his eyes again. "Too real," he mumbled as he sat up. Looking around, Michael saw that he was on a concrete floor surrounded by . . . paper?

Sitting up straight, he rubbed his eyes as his senses cleared. Directly in front of him was more paper. Michael rolled to his knees and got to his feet. He saw that these were not ordinary pieces of white paper but photographs. All the photographs were of children-—children of all ages and colors. Banded sets of photographs were stacked neatly on shelf after shelf after shelf.

Michael stepped into an opening on his left. It was an aisle of some sort, and just beyond it stood massive racks of clothing. Walking over to one rack, he ran his hand over a small coat. He realized quickly that every single article of clothing was a coat. *Thousands*, Michael thought, maybe even *hundreds of thousands*.

Michael turned back toward the photographs and gasped. There were shelves of photographs one on top of another stacked literally out of sight. Looking up, he couldn't even see a ceiling.

There were no light fixtures in the place, or any lights for that matter, and yet, somehow, everything was bathed in a soft, even glow. To his right and left, the aisles continued without end. There seemed to be no definite structure to the building, if it was, in fact, a building at all. *Am I still dreaming?* Michael wondered.

He kept walking and found new aisles, but none with an end. He saw blue jeans and medicine and pictures of homes. There were heaters and diplomas, marriage licenses, bicycle tires, and food. Slowly, he worked his way back to the pictures of the children.

On the way, he passed an area stacked with money—cash from all over the world in all amounts. "This makes absolutely no sense," he said aloud. Continuing down the aisle, he counted two hundred and nine steps before the money was no longer beside him.

Soon, Michael was back where he had begun, even though he knew he hadn't even seen close to everything. As he turned in a complete circle, gazing all around him, a picture fluttered down from somewhere above. It landed on the floor not far from where Michael stood. Picking it up, he moved to place it back on a shelf, but stopped. Something bothered him about the photograph.

It was a color photo of two children, a boy and a girl, each around nine or ten years old. They were obviously brother and sister and looked very similar to Michael. He shook his head in wonder.

Faintly, almost as if it was in his head, Michael heard something. Glancing up, he looked down the aisle and saw a figure walking toward him. Michael was tall, but this man would clearly tower over him. He had blond, almost golden, curly hair. It touched his eyebrows and barely brushed his ears. He was wearing a robe that draped over his shoulders and hung to his knees. It was white, or maybe light. In fact, this man seemed to be dressed in what Michael could only describe as shades of light.

The man smiled a greeting as he came closer, then stopped and turned to straighten a wheelchair on his right. When he did, Michael's mouth dropped open. The man had wings!

Closing the distance between them, the man stopped and said, "Hello, Michael Holder. I am Gabriel."

Michael stared at him in awe. "You're an angel," he finally managed to say.

"An archangel actually." Gabriel smiled, revealing perfectly even, white teeth. "There is a difference, you know."

"I'm sorry, I . . . ahh . . . I really didn't," Michael stammered. "Know, I mean. That there was a difference."

"No matter, Michael Holder," Gabriel responded. "I am honored to make your acquaintance."

Pointing to the photograph Michael still had in his hand, he said, "May I?"

"Oh . . . sure!" Michael said and gave it to him.

Gabriel looked at the picture for a moment. "Beautiful children, aren't they?" Michael nodded in agreement and watched as Gabriel placed it in the basket of loose photos.

"So I *am* dead?" Michael blurted out.

Gabriel wrinkled his forehead and appeared confused. "Excuse me?"

"If I'm with you, then I must be in heaven, right? And if I'm in heaven, I must be dead."

Gabriel laughed. "No, you are not dead. This is merely a stopover, perhaps the most important stopover in your travels. This is the only destination that all travelers have in common."

"Have there been many travelers?" Michael asked.

"Relatively few," Gabriel said, "when one considers the beginning of time as you know it and the number of people with whom we have dealt. But for those who are chosen to travel, an understanding of their true mission begins here, in this place. Joan of Arc, George Washington, and Martin Luther King, Jr. all took a step toward destiny from where you now stand."

"Which is where exactly?" Michael motioned with his hands. "What is this place?"

Gabriel held up one finger. "Not quite yet," he said. "First, let us walk together." Moving slowly, Gabriel led Michael past ceiling fans and air conditioners, tires and blankets, watches and pictures of animals.

As they walked, Michael asked the angel, "Why am I here?"

Gabriel smiled. "Why do you think you're here?"

"I don't know," Michael answered.

"Then it is not time for you to know," Gabriel said. "Come."

Pointing to a piece of machinery, Michael asked, "What is this?"

"That bit of equipment," Gabriel responded, "renders any moveable object collision-proof. The design is a combination of laser and sound-wave technology effective on anything from automobiles to jumbo jets."

Michael thought of his friend still in the hospital who would have benefited from such a machine. He ran his fingers through his hair and asked, "If you won't tell me what this place is and you won't say why I am here, then let me ask you a different question." Gabriel nodded. "Why are all these things here?"

Brushing his hand over one of the many vacuum cleaners they were walking by, Gabriel appeared deep in thought. "What is the difference in people, Michael Holder," the angel began, "when they hit despair? Why does one person give up on life while another moves on to greatness?"

"That didn't really answer my question," Michael replied, "but I'm not sure. I've never really thought about it."

Gabriel turned, still walking, with a mildly amused look on his face. "Think about it now," he said.

Michael shrugged. "I don't know. Maybe a difference in circumstances?"

"Circumstances are rulers of the weak," Gabriel said, "but they are weapons of the wise. Must you be torn by every situation you encounter?" Michael frowned as the angel pressed on. "That is a question, Michael Holder. Are your emotions and strength controlled by circumstances?"

"No, they are not," Michael said firmly.

"That is correct." Gabriel nodded. "Circumstances do not push or pull. They are daily lessons to be studied for new knowledge and wisdom. Knowledge and wisdom that is applied will bring about a brighter tomorrow. A frustrated person is spending too much time thinking about how things are now and not enough time about how he wants things to be."

Michael thought for a minute and swung his arm toward an area filled with mattresses. "So why are all of these things here?"

Gabriel glanced up at his confused pupil briefly and said, "Circumstances."

Michael sighed loudly. Gabriel laughed and said, "Walk this way, Michael Holder."

Michael followed the angel down an aisle lined with telephones on one side and lumber on the other. Soon they were back to Michael's starting place, the area with the photographs of children. "Have I seen it all?" Michael asked.

"You have seen only a tiny fraction of this facility," Gabriel answered. "A lifetime of wandering would not cover it all. And sadly, it gets bigger every day."

Michael stopped near the baskets of loose pictures. Reaching in, he removed the one Gabriel had placed there earlier—the one with the two children Michael had found so familiar. "The boy's name is Patrick," Gabriel said quietly. "The girl is Natalie."

Still looking at the photo, Michael remarked, "That's funny. My mom always said if I was a girl, they were going to name me Natalie. I can remember my parents talking about having another child, but they couldn't afford it. I always wanted a brother or . . ." Michael stopped abruptly. "But you already knew that, didn't you?"

"Yes," Gabriel answered.

"Why is this happening to me?" Michael asked.

Gabriel's eyes narrowed. "Explain yourself more clearly, please."

"Why am I seeing this now?"

"Special dispensation is allowed for a traveler to gain greater wisdom and understanding."

"I don't understand."

"Obviously."

Michael took a deep breath. "Am I *supposed* to somehow understand?"

"Everything will become clear to you."

As Michael continued to look all around him, trying to absorb everything the angel had said, his attention strayed toward a single, small pedestal that was illumined by a bright light. On the pedestal was a stack of papers not even a quarter of an inch high. "Hey, where is the light coming from?" he asked. Gabriel only smiled. Michael moved closer. "May I touch this?"

"Certainly," Gabriel responded.

There were forty or fifty sheets of paper, some newer, some yellowed with age, in the pile. Michael flipped through the papers and saw mathematical equations, blueprints, and one with only one word in the middle. He turned to Gabriel. "What are these?"

"One of them," Gabriel said, "is plans for a machine that will regenerate the optic nerve, allowing even those who are blind from birth to see." He paused and looked straight into Michael's eyes. "Page nine is the cure for lung cancer."

Michael was stunned. "Am I supposed to take these?"

"No," Gabriel said.

Angry and confused, Michael sputtered, "Then why . . . ?!" He couldn't find the words. Michael slammed the papers down on the pedestal and ignored the crack in his voice as he said too loudly, "What is going on? All these things . . . these cures . . . my dad is in the hospital with lung cancer. Did you know that?"

"Yes."

This was more than Michael could stand. "What kind of a cruel joke is this?" he shouted. "Are you telling me that my father may be dying and you have the cure right here, and you aren't going to do anything about it?!"

Pain and sadness and frustration seemed to rise out of his soul at that very moment. He collapsed on the ground and wept bitterly. He cried for his mom and dad. He missed them. Would he ever see them again? Did he deserve to? He cried for the people he had let down in his life—his parents, his friends, his teachers—and he cried for himself.

Tears still flowing down his face, Michael looked up at Gabriel and asked, "Please help me understand. Please tell me, what is this place?"

Gabriel took a step closer to Michael and swept out his arms as if to present an honored guest. "This, my friend, is the place that never was. This is the place where we keep all the things that were about to be delivered just as a person stopped working and praying for them. This warehouse is filled with the dreams and goals of the less courageous."

Michael was horrified. He looked up and down the aisle at the coats and shoes, bicycles and blankets, the cures and designs on the pedestal. So many hopes and dreams that were never realized. Michael thought of the countless times he had longed for something, hoped for something, and then had just given up, either on himself or on someone else. How many times had he been too lazy or too easily discouraged? What opportunities had he already missed? What could have belonged to him in this room that he would now never have?

Remembering the picture of the brother and sister he would never know, Michael asked, "May I at least keep the picture?"

"I'm sorry," the angel said, "but Patrick and Natalie do not exist. The time for their arrival has passed. The opportunity is missed. There are no second chances."

After sitting quietly for a while, his head resting on his knees, Michael finally looked up and asked in a weak voice, "What am I supposed to learn here?"

Gabriel smiled and sat down beside Michael on the floor. "You must know," he began, "that in the game of life, the tragedy is not that a man loses, but that he *almost wins*."

Michael shook his head slowly. "Why do I—why does anyone—give up?"

Gabriel responded instantly, "As a human, you detour and give up because you lack understanding. You quit because you lack faith."

"Understanding about what?"

"For one thing, you do not understand that constant detours do not bring a man into the presence of greatness. Between you and anything significant will be giants in your path. Most slow down when the road appears treacherous. But these are the times when you must feel the weight of your future on your shoulders. Times of calamity and distress have always been producers of the greatest men."

For a while, Michael was silent, deep in thought. Then after locking away the angel's words, he said, "Gabriel, you also mentioned that I lacked faith. What did you mean by that?"

"I meant your race. The human race. With only a few exceptions, you lack the faith that produces greatness." Gabriel sighed. "It was not always so. Your civilization was once alive, vibrant, productive, and borne in glory. Now look at you—a wandering, questioning pack of rebels teetering on the brink of dissolution."

"What?" Michael couldn't believe his ears. "We are living in the most advanced age the planet has ever seen!"

Gabriel shook his head sadly. "You truly have no memory or knowledge of your history. There once existed a culture on earth so highly evolved as to make you look like dull children. Their mathematics, engineering, and architecture were far beyond what you have today. These were people of great understanding, great wisdom, and an even greater faith."

"Why have we never heard of these people?" Michael asked doubtfully.

"Because most of your scientists work within a parameter of time that is far too narrow. A few of them, however, have begun to suspect that this society predated the Aztecs and Incas by more than thirty thousand of your years. Your civilization is just now arriving at the point of recognizing the scant clues still left of their existence."

"What clues?"

Gabriel paused for a moment, then said, "The engineering of Cuencan temples, still standing in what you call South America, used stones that weigh more than one hundred tons each. The builders of Balbek in Lebanon laid cornerstones as tall as your five-story buildings. They weigh more than six hundred tons apiece.

"In both places—and many more, I might add—the blocks were quarried and set together so perfectly that grout was never considered necessary. Just to cut stone to the same specifications, your engineers today require diamond-tipped, laser-guided quarry saws. And still, they can't duplicate the dimensions.

"And that is just the beginning. Their knowledge of astronomy also far exceeded your current levels. They knew the exact circumference of the earth and chartered it into systems of measure around the world. This is now evident in surviving buildings in South America and Europe because they incorporated the figures into their architecture. You were able to obtain these exact mathematical values only after Sputnik circled the earth in 1957.

"Truth needs no evidence, of course." Gabriel smiled.

"But since you were curious, that should give you something to consider."

Michael tried to comprehend the existence of such a culture. "Why are they gone?" he asked.

"For the same reasons that your civilization is in trouble," Gabriel said carefully. "Arrogance, ungratefulness, and a loss of faith. Your people have reached the edge of the same cliff in an astonishingly short time."

"Is there anything we can do to change?"

"Of course," Gabriel said. "And that is precisely why you are here." Gabriel stood and helped Michael to his feet. Reaching into the folds of his robe, the angel withdrew a small scroll. He extended it to Michael and said, "This decision is the final portion of the whole. Take it."

As Michael took the scroll in his hand, Gabriel frowned. "I am not certain why you were selected for this great honor, Michael Holder, for I am but a messenger." He paused. "You are the last traveler. There will not be another. You have been given a gift that has the power to change your civilization. Everything from this moment on will depend upon you.

"You will study one decision at a time, each for twenty-one days. You will read it aloud twice daily during that time. First, upon wakening, and again, as the last thing you do before sleep. You must not miss a day. Each decision will become part of you, buried in your heart, captured in your soul.

"You will share the gift of the decisions with others. Those who absorb and apply this wisdom will rise to greatness and inspire others to the same heights."

Gabriel placed his hands on each side of Michael's face. "You have everything you need, Michael Holder. You know that you are not alone. You are being guided. There will never be a reason to lose faith. The future is yours. But be warned. Yours is a future as you choose it. Our Creator has granted you the extraordinary power of the wisdom contained in the Seven Decisions. But He also grants you free will. Should you choose to ignore this power, the future will be lost forever.

"You will be granted one more journey, Michael Holder. It is a rare gift, indeed. You have come to this place and seen all the things that never were, and now you will have the chance to see what might be. But be warned, it is only a hope, only a possibility. The choices you make from this moment forward will shape and define your future; you have the power to make things happen; you have the ability to change the world, Michael Holder—if you so choose."

Michael took Gabriel's hands in his own and said, "Thank you. I will make the very most of this gift."

"Yes, Michael Holder," he said, "I believe that you will." And with those words, he slowly stretched his wings over his head, and in a thunderous rush of wind, flew up and was gone.

For a few moments, Michael stood there, watching and thinking. Then slowly, he began a purposeful walk. He glanced around to memorize this place and what it meant. Then he eased down onto the floor and unrolled the scroll of Gabriel.

The Seventh Decision for Success

I will persist without exception.

Knowing that I have already made changes in my life that will last forever, today I insert the final piece of the puzzle. I possess the greatest power ever bestowed upon humankind, the power of choice. Today, I choose to persist without exception. No longer will I be distracted, my focus blowing with the wind. I know the outcome I want. I will hold fast to my dreams. I will stay the course. I do not quit.

I will persist without exception. I will continue despite exhaustion.

I know that most people quit when exhaustion sets in. I am not "most people." I am stronger than most people. Average people give in to exhaustion. I do not. Average people compare themselves with other people. That is why they are average. I compare myself to my potential. I am not average. I see exhaustion as a precursor to victory.

I will persist without exception. I will focus on results.

To achieve the results I desire, it is not even necessary

that I enjoy the process. It is only important that I continue the process with my eyes on the outcome. An athlete does not enjoy the pain of training; an athlete enjoys the results of having trained.

I will persist without exception. I am a person of great faith.

In Jeremiah, my Creator declares, "I know the plans I have for you, plans to prosper you and not to harm you, plans to give you hope and a future." From this day forward, I will have faith in my future. I will believe in the future that I do not see. That is faith. And the reward of this faith is to one day see the future that I believed in.

I will continue despite exhaustion. I will focus on results. I am a person of great faith.

I will persist without exception.

ten

Michael took a deep breath and exhaled loudly. Carefully he rolled up the scroll. Then, standing, he fished the canvas pouch from his blue jeans pocket. Michael traced the embroidery of crossed swords on the flap. *The symbol of a fighting man,* he thought. *I am not a quitter. I am a fighting man.* Suddenly, Michael smiled. "I will persist without exception," he said aloud.

Quickly, he carefully added the scroll to the other pages of knowledge in his pouch. "Thank you," he murmured as he put the pouch back in his pocket. He was overwhelmed by thoughts of the people he had met. Then Michael stopped. Remembering the larger picture, he closed his eyes, bowed his head, and said the same words again, "Thank *You*."

Opening his eyes, Michael found himself in a large parking lot. He almost laughed out loud at his *lack* of surprise. He didn't know where he was but realized that he wasn't afraid or even unsure of himself. He wondered if he'd ever be shocked by anything again!

It was nighttime, but the lights of the parking lot helped him to weave his way through the cars. He seemed to be drawn to a building at the other end of the lot, and he began making his way toward the entrance. As he walked, he looked up and immediately recognized the skyline. His heart skipped a beat. The Reunion Tower, the Magnolia Building, the National Bank—all told Michael he was home.

Staring up at the skyscrapers, Michael almost fell over the car in front of him. "Whoaaa." He let out a slow breath as he examined the fine piece of machinery. The Jaguar emblem on the hood was unmistakable, but the rest of the car was unlike any Jaguar he'd ever seen. As he looked down the row of cars, he realized that *none* of them was like any cars he'd ever seen.

"I'm in the future," he said to himself and began walking even faster toward the building that seemed to call his name. As he got closer, he was able to make out the words across the arch of the entrance: Auditorium for Literary Sciences. *Ohhh, so I will* make it to college, huh? he thought, smiling to himself.

Slowly, he walked toward the entrance and approached the woman at the booth. "Excuse me, ma'am. Ma'am?" She seemed to look right through him. *I guess I can't be seen in the future either,* Michael thought.

As he made his way through the front door, an usher stopped him in his tracks. "Oh, good evening, Mr. Holder. We weren't aware that you'd be coming tonight."

Mr. Holder? Nice school—such respect for their students, such personal treatment. Michael was surprised by the usher's behavior, but this was obviously a man put here to help him see his future.

"Right this way, sir." The man led Michael to a long corridor where he stopped at an elevator door and motioned for Michael to step inside. The usher pulled out a key and inserted it into the keyhole beside a star.

When the elevator chimed and the doors opened, the usher stood at the door, making the way for Michael to pass. "Thank you," Michael said, and the usher stepped back onto the elevator with a slight bow.

"Nice guy," Michael said to himself as the elevator doors closed. Looking around, he found himself in a modern, half-circle hallway with large windows overlooking an auditorium. Michael had a bird's-eye view of the speaker and the crowd in front of him. *Man,* that *place is packed!* he thought as he looked out over the group.

Michael walked down the hallway and stopped dead in front of a brass doorplate with "Michael Holder" engraved in large letters. *Okay. Coincidence?* he asked himself. He tried to turn the doorknob, but it was locked. *Too weird,* he thought and continued walking.

At the end of the hallway was a door marked "Stairs." He opened the door and walked down the flight of stairs. When he reached the bottom, he opened another door and found himself behind rows and rows of people. This door was obviously an entrance into the auditorium he had seen from the hallway windows above.

A young man was speaking up front. "I was on the bench in front of the Literary Building with tears running down my face. I didn't know what to do or where to turn. Then, Mr. Holder . . . Michael just walked up and sat down beside me. He shared the First Decision with me, handed me a worn copy of the book, and helped me to straighten things out. I wouldn't be here today if it weren't for that man."

The crowd cheered. Michael had to sit down. *Could they be talking about me? What could I have done to make him cry like that in front of his friends?*

He looked at the sea of people sitting in the audience and noticed that many of them were holding the same book. Then he saw it. At first, he thought it was a picture of his father on the book jacket. No, it wasn't his father. Definitely not. He leaned over and peered closer at the book in the teenage girl's hand in front of him. He stifled a gasp. There, on the back of the book, Michael caught a glimpse of himself—well, himself with a little less hair— staring back at him!

Instantly, Michael knew what he had to do. He turned around, grabbed the doorknob, and sprang through the door. He ran and ran, all the way down the stairs until he reached the bottom level. He burst out the door, looked left, and ran toward the Exit sign.

The same usher that had carried him up on the elevator shouted, "Sir?! Sir?! Is there something wrong?"

"No! No! Not at all! Everything is wonderful! Crystal clear!" Michael yelled, running toward the door.

"Y-y-yes. Yes, sir." The usher stepped aside as Michael dashed through the doors.

"Thank you!" Michael yelled without turning back.

Michael Holder ran. He ran with a purpose. He ran with a vision. He ran until he could not run any longer. He stopped, breathless, and rested by a tree in the parking lot. Collapsing to his knees, and then leaning back to a sitting position, Michael wondered how to get home. He rested his head against the tree, suddenly overwhelmed by exhaustion. His eyes became heavier and heavier. He tried to fight it. He had to tell his mom, had to see his dad, had to start now. . . . But the darkness enveloped him and Michael Holder drifted to sleep.

eleven

ichael? Honey? Can you hear me?" Michael's vision was blurry as he tried to focus on the person in front of him.

He heard another voice, a man. "It may take some time, Mrs. Holder." Everyone sounded so far away.

"Michael, it's Mom. I'm right here."

Michael felt a warm drop of liquid land on his arm, and he looked up into his mother's eyes.

Mom? Michael could hear the simple question in his

head, but the sound that came out was just an inaudible murmur.

"Michael, you stay right here. You hear me? Stay with me." His mom's voice was desperate, pleading.

He tried to grab her hand, but his arm wouldn't obey. His vision and hearing seemed to come and go, closer and farther, softer and louder.

"Mom?" This time the question came out, and he looked up to focus on her face. "Mom, I'm okay."

"Oh, yes, Michael. Yes, honey, you're okay. You're going to be just fine."

"No, I mean, I'm going to be okay. My future. I, I don't know how I'll pay for college, but I'll figure it out. I have hope. I have vision. I saw places you'd never . . ."

"Whoa, there, young man." The doctor put his hand on Michael's shoulder. "You'll have plenty of time to explain. Rest for now."

"Dad? How's Dad?"

"He's doing great, honey." Michael's mom smiled the biggest smile he had seen on her face in a long time. "He's doing wonderfully. The surgery was a success."

Michael smiled. In a matter of seconds, Michael's head cleared and his vision sharpened. He looked around and, seeing his mom and a short man in a white coat huddled over him, asked, "Where am I?"

"You're in the hospital, son," his mom answered. "You were in an accident."

"Am I . . . ?"

"You will recover, Michael." The short man moved forward. "I'm Dr. Green. You are a very lucky young man."

"I . . . I went down an embankment."

"Yes, you did," the doctor replied. "And the fact that you can remember anything at all is a very good sign. You have a severe concussion. Do you remember anything else?"

"I had been at the Literary Building."

His mom tilted her head. "No, honey, you were going to look for a job."

The doctor placed his hand on her shoulder. "Mrs. Holder, don't worry, his thoughts will be jumbled for a while." He smiled at Michael and shrugged. "That is one nasty lick to the head you have, but all in all, you are in very good shape. I can honestly say I've never seen anything like it. The paramedics said you'd been thrown from the car, and we haven't found as much as a broken bone. Yes sir, I'd say that you were one extremely lucky young man."

eleven

As the doctor went on about what to expect as Michael healed and which medicines he would prescribe, Michael looked over at his mom. Yes, he was one lucky young man. His dad was recovering well. His mom was by his side. And he, Michael Holder, had a future, a bright future ahead of him.

Then, a bit of disappointment set over him. Was it all just a dream? It had seemed real. He felt like he had been there! He could feel the warm air on his face in Potsdam. He could smell the musty attic in Amsterdam. And he certainly felt the seasickness on board the *Santa Maria*. But no one would ever believe him, Michael knew, and he wasn't sure he believed it himself.

But that's not important, Michael thought. *What did I learn? Even if it had been a dream, did those Seven Decisions have less value?* Michael smiled as he recalled the words of each key phrase.

"Michael, honey?" Michael looked up from his thoughts. "I'm going over to tell Dad you're awake. He's just down the hall in a regular room now."

Michael couldn't wait to see his dad. He had so much to tell him . . . and his forgiveness to ask.

"Wait, Mom."

"Yes, Michael?"

"I'm sorry."

"It was forgiven in an instant."

"Thanks, Mom." Michael smiled. "Oh, and Mom?"

"Yes, Michael?"

"Do you have any paper?"

"I believe there's some in your backpack. They brought it with you in the ambulance. The clothes you were wearing are in there too." His mom picked up the bag and laid it gently on Michael's bed. "For you, my dahling," she said in her exaggerated British accent.

Michael grinned.

"Need anything else?" she asked.

"Nope. I have all I need."

Michael's mom blew him a kiss as she walked out the door. Michael watched until the door was completely closed, then feverishly began searching his backpack for paper. He pulled out a notebook and reached back in to search the depths of the bag for a pen.

As he dug through the candy wrappers and paper wads, a familiar texture brushed his hand. Michael stopped and held the item in his hand. Tears welled up in his eyes as he removed a small, canvas pouch.

eleven

It was navy blue and had been sewn from stout cloth, but the rough treatment it had received had worn the pouch to a moleskin softness. It was beaten and thread-bare, but still handsome, regal in a sense, the possession of an officer. The two gold buttons that closed the flap were metal, engraved with the image of an eagle. And there, just above the buttons, embroidered on the flap, were crossed swords, the symbol of a fighting man.

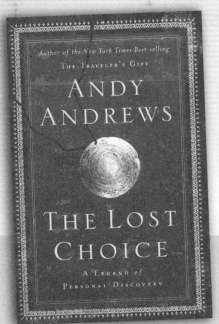